THE
SUMMER
REUNION

BOOKS BY LEAH MERCER

A Mother's Lie
Why She Left
A Secret in the Family
The Mother Next Door
The Playgroup

Who We Were Before
The Man I Thought You Were
The Puzzle of You
Ten Little Words

THE
SUMMER
REUNION

LEAH MERCER

bookouture

Published by Bookouture in 2024

An imprint of Storyfire Ltd.
Carmelite House
50 Victoria Embankment
London EC4Y 0DZ

www.bookouture.com

ISBN: 978-1-83525-571-1
eBook ISBN: 978-1-83525-570-4

*For my mother, who has always supported and encouraged me,
no matter how far off-track I have travelled.*

PROLOGUE

She crouched in the dark, the only sound the trickle of water as it flowed into the cramped cellar. The dank liquid had already reached her waist and was rising quickly. If she didn't get out of here soon... She *had* to get out of here soon. There must be a key somewhere, with someone.

She glanced at the man on a crate beside her. Was he the enemy she'd always believed? Or was the real enemy outside – someone she'd trusted for years? Someone she'd *loved* for years? Uncertainty swirled around her. All she'd believed for so long had crumbled into darkness, threatening to engulf her like the black water.

Thunder boomed above as the storm got stronger, and his eyes met hers. She wanted to look away, but she couldn't. She wanted to run, but she was trapped. Trapped in this place that she'd been trying to escape... not just now, but for years.

She never should have come back. She should have stayed far, far away. But it was too late for regrets. She was here, and they were together.

And as the water kept rising, she didn't know whether to be comforted by that – or terrified.

ONE

ELLIE

'Look at this place. Nothing has changed in twenty years.' Ellie Kovic dropped the heavy case she was dragging and stared at the villa in front of her. Red flowers danced in the soft spring breeze, and vines climbed up the worn stone blocks of the house. Ellie would ask Jules the name of the flowers when she arrived; she always knew. The earthy scent from nearby vineyards wrapped around her, and instantly she was transported back to when all five of them had come here to celebrate finishing university. Hard to believe it had been twenty years! They'd had such a great time back then that a few months ago Ellie had dared to suggest they make good on their promise to return for a reunion. And now, after much organising on her part, the weekend was here.

'You haven't changed a bit either.' Safet put his hands on her shoulders, and she turned to smile at him. She knew he meant his words as a compliment, but she hoped she *had* changed – that she was no longer the mousy girl in the background, trailing behind the glamorous, gorgeous Jules and her best friend, Vannie, who'd always brimmed with confidence.

She took a deep breath, smoothing her sundress and

pushing back the sleek dark hair that had taken ages to straighten this morning before they'd left for the airport. As she'd gazed in the mirror, she'd thought that for the first time she would actually feel OK standing beside elegant Jules or vibrant Vannie, rather than being a pale imitation who was trying too hard.

If only she could have convinced Safet to change from his black T-shirt and jeans, she thought, gazing at her husband. Ever since she'd known him, this had been his daily uniform. The one and only time he'd actually dressed up was for their wedding. She'd bought him some linen trousers and a nice shirt to wear today, but they'd stayed on the bed, untouched.

'Who am I trying to impress?' he'd asked as he threw on his usual outfit. 'You know I don't care about that.'

Ellie might have doubted the words from anyone else, but from her husband she believed them. Although he'd seemed shy and uncertain that first year they'd all shared a suite in the student halls, once she'd got to know him he'd had a quiet confidence she'd always admired. Both more apt to stay in reading than partying, they'd grown close quickly, their relationship blossoming from friendship to romance when Safet had kissed her, taking her by surprise. She smiled, remembering how she'd been about to ask him what he wanted from the supermarket, when he'd stepped forward and put his lips on hers. It hadn't *really* been a surprise, but she'd been afraid to believe he liked her that way. He'd stayed by her side, moving with the group from the halls to a house off-campus, and then moving as a couple to London. They'd made a wonderful life together.

She could tell by his stoic expression that this was the last place he wanted to be. He'd come, though, even after asking why they should travel all this way to be with people they rarely saw. She'd laughed, saying once you'd lived with someone at university, you were bonded for life. Spending those years filled with firsts and heady freedom together was an experience they could never forget, no matter how far they drifted. Why wouldn't they want the chance to relive it?

Besides, she couldn't wait for their group to see what a fantastic life she had. Somehow, it had always felt as if she was the one least likely to succeed. She made a face. Given that she'd graduated with a useless sociology degree, that had seemed probable. But with a handsome husband, two great children and a job she loved that also helped others, it actually felt as if she'd won the life lottery.

'Hey, guys.' She put her arms around her kids, Victoria and Ahmed, as they came running up behind her. 'Ready to go inside?'

She knocked on the huge wooden door, and a smiling man swung it open. She'd arranged for the property manager to meet them so she could get the lay of the land before the others arrived. The kids gasped as they took in the huge, vaulted ceiling and the winding staircase, and Ellie grinned, remembering her first awed reaction. She'd grown up in a three-bedroom semi, and this kind of living was foreign to her. She'd never have been able to afford it back then if Jules's father hadn't treated them all to the trip. Even now, she'd had to dip into some savings so they could go. It had been ages since they'd had a family holiday, though. This would be worth it.

'Let me show you where everything is,' the property manager was saying. 'Then I'll get out of your way and let you enjoy your weekend.'

'Perfect. Thank you.' Ellie glanced around, thinking she probably hadn't needed the manager, after all. So far, the place was exactly as she remembered. 'Kids, what do you think? Nice, huh?'

'Is that a pool?' Victoria twisted from her grasp and dashed towards the water without waiting for a response, while Ahmed clung to her side. Even after two years with the family, the eleven-year-old still acted like he could be torn from them at any moment... not that she blamed him after what had happened to his family back in his native Syria. Once the adoption order went through, he could relax and believe he was with them for good. They *all* could relax. The endless delays were killing them.

She bit her lip as she looked at her husband tapping on his phone, his leg jiggling as if hooked up to electricity. Hopefully, this trip would let them unwind and enjoy being together.

Ellie sighed as she watched Victoria dip her feet in the pool, her lovely long dark hair falling like a curtain over her face. Ever since they'd taken in Ahmed, their daughter had pulled away from them. She used to tell Ellie everything, but now Victoria spent most of her time in her room, flicking off the screen whenever Ellie came inside to check what she was up to. When she told Safet she was worried, though, he said it was normal behaviour for a girl her age. Ellie hoped he was right.

She smiled at Ahmed as he stared towards the pool. He was learning to love the water even though he still couldn't swim.

'You're not to go in here without your water wings and someone nearby, OK?'

Ahmed nodded. 'I won't. I promise.'

Ellie put a hand on his shoulder. He was such a good boy, although sometimes she wondered if he was *too* good – if his behaviour was powered by fear. He seemed to have found a way to cope with the world, though: by filming everything on the old mobile Safet had given him. Ellie had questioned whether it was healthy for him to have it so much, but Safet had explained that filming was Ahmed's way of placing a filter between himself and the reality of a strange world he still found threatening. He'd been born at the start of the violence in his country and lived his whole life in a warzone. Fear was all he knew. In time, he'd put the phone down.

'Mum!' Victoria's voice echoed off the stone walls.

Ellie and Ahmed followed the property manager across the

cobbled patio and towards an outbuilding that was off to the side of the main villa. Ellie was about to ask if this was new when the manager mentioned it was an old storage shed they'd recently converted. She didn't remember it being here before, but this whole place was littered with random structures, a remnant of the days when it was a working vineyard, and they'd barely strayed from the villa last time.

She poked her head into the building, taking in the spacious lounge and high ceilings. The place was kitted out with a full kitchen and what looked like three or four bedrooms.

'Mum, can I stay in here?' Victoria looked ecstatic at the thought of being off her mother's lead.

Ellie paused, not liking the thought of Victoria so far away from her. She was fourteen, though, and as Safet kept telling her, she needed more independence. Jules's girls would likely want to stay here too. They could all watch out for each other.

'That's fine, I guess,' she said in response to Victoria. 'As long as you don't stay up all night.'

Victoria rolled her eyes. 'At least I'll be away from him. Creep.' She shot Ahmed a hard look before turning away to investigate the rooms.

Their son shrank back against Ellie's side as if the words were a physical blow.

Ellie sighed. 'Victoria, come—'

Safet came up behind her. 'Let her go,' he said quietly. 'They'll connect in their own time.'

Ellie nodded, hoping once more that he was right. She waved goodbye to the property manager, then turned towards her husband, excitement building. This place was theirs now. The weekend started here.

'Should we go find our own room, then? Same one?' She smiled, remembering how magical that first visit had been. They'd been together for three years at that point, ever since their first year at Uni. Ellie had loved every single minute with

Safet, unable to resist fantasising about weddings and babies. She'd never known for sure if Safet pictured her in his future, though, and she'd been terrified to bring it up. When they'd sat by the pool the final night of their stay, he'd asked her if she'd go to London with him and start a life there. She'd been so happy she'd barely been able to speak.

'Anyone here?' Jules's voice bounced around the villa.

Ellie noticed how Safet instantly perked up. Jules had that effect on everyone.

'Honeys, we're home!' Harry's voice boomed out next.

Safet grimaced. He wasn't the biggest fan of Jules's husband, but she hoped they could get on this weekend. She hoped they *all* could get on, like they had twenty years ago.

'It will be OK,' she told her husband, even as she felt Ahmed gripping her tighter. 'Relax, have a drink. I can't wait to catch up and remember all the crazy times we had. Come on, let's go say hi.'

Truthfully, though, she'd never really had crazy times. She'd had Safet, and he'd been more than enough for her.

TWO
JULES

'God, this place hasn't changed, has it? You'd think they'd at least try to update it.' Harry's muscles strained as he lifted the twins' cases from the car boot, and Jules prayed he wouldn't bust out of the new shirt she'd bought him. It was meant to be a slim fit, but now the buttons seemed about to pop. The terra-cotta colour would look perfect with his salt-and-pepper hair as he posed against the creamy stone blocks of the villa, though, if he could only keep it together. Despite the years that had passed, like the property, he hadn't changed much either – although maybe she should have bought that shirt one size bigger.

'Girls. *Girls!*' She yanked open the car door, sighing as she tried to get their attention. Their fifteen-year-old twins had the high-end headphones Harry had bought them clamped over their ears as they watched someone dancing on TikTok – although to Jules's eyes, it looked more like a strip show than an entertaining video. According to Mia and Nat, though, that was normal and Jules was the worst prude ever.

They both looked up at her as if she was nothing more than

a bug to swat away. 'We're here, guys. Ellie and her family are here too. Come say hello.'

Nat rolled her eyes and got out of the car. 'Not that weirdo kid who hardly talks and films everything.' They'd met Ahmed once when Jules had volunteered at a fundraiser Safet and Ellie organised for the refugee charity they worked for. The twins' mum had foisted them on Harry before jetting off on holiday somewhere, and, as usual, Harry had passed the buck to her. Being a stepmum was hard enough, but when those kids were the result of an affair...

'Nat!' Jules shook her head. 'I told you about his background. You could be a bit more sensitive.'

'Dad says he can't wait until the next government comes to power and then we can stop people from coming here when they shouldn't,' Mia parroted what she'd heard Harry say.

Jules felt a rush of anger go through her. How could Harry, who lived such a comfortable life, have such selfish thoughts? And how could he spread them like that, especially knowing what both Safet and Ahmed had been through? It was true he and Safet had never been close – they were polar opposites – but Harry knew how hard Safet had worked to make something of himself after fleeing Bosnia as a young teen.

She smiled as she thought of Safet. Hopefully, they could sit down this weekend and *talk*, beyond the texts and calls they'd exchanged the past few weeks. She'd seen him a few times over the years at events for his charity, and she'd admired how his gentle but assertive nature calmed even the most challenging children. He'd really made something of himself. Ellie had, too, if you believed the annual newsletter she persistently emailed each year at Christmas. Funny how the two of them had always been the ones in the background at Uni, and now they were being invited to garden parties at Buckingham Palace to honour their work, shaking hands with the royals. She sighed, picturing

Ellie bowing and scraping as Safet stood like a soldier by her side.

God, she couldn't wait to spend more time with him. With Harry away for work and their daughter Ivy in her studio flat in Notting Hill, Jules had needed something besides wine o'clock to help fill the hours. Not that her life wasn't fine as it was, of course. She'd never do anything to upset it, but there were only so many photos of dewy wine glasses, vibrant flowerpots or yummy-mummy outfits she could take, and she was starting to feel a little bored.

More and more, her mind would drift back to those first few weeks at Uni, every memory seeming in techni-colour... where the possibilities had been endless. Before she and Harry had got together, she'd loved flirting with the boys, enjoying how they'd look at her with desire. One evening early on, everyone in their suite had been out except for her and Safet. He'd been reading in the common area, and she'd plunked down beside him, trying to engage him with her usual banter that worked so well.

He'd glanced up and simply said he was reading, but that she was welcome to join him. Normally, she'd have flounced off with an eye-roll, but something about his calmness had appealed. She'd brought out a book and, together, they'd sat for hours until the suite came to life again. Sometimes, when she was sitting alone at home now, she couldn't help thinking back to that night. So, heart pounding, she'd reached out to Safet a few months back and they'd started chatting.

When Ellie's proposal of a weekend reunion at the villa slid into her DMs, she'd leapt at the chance to go. Harry would relish lounging by the pool and drinking for two days straight, and she and Safet could finally see each other in real life; finally see where this could take her. She bit her lip, thinking it wasn't great going behind Ellie's back – or Harry's, for that matter – but it wouldn't be forever. She did kind of like the feeling of having something all to herself, though... of dreaming of the future once again.

How ironic that this would happen in a place where she had such terrible memories – memories of when she'd dared to dream of the future too. Dream of a different life with a man she'd connected with like no other, not even Harry. A man she knew she could really love, if she'd had the chance.

But that chance had been taken away before she could even begin to grasp it.

Frederick's face floated into her mind, and she jerked at the pain that hit like a physical blow. After her mother had died in their last year of Uni, Harry hadn't been able to deal with her grief – not that she could blame him, she couldn't either. Even her best friend Vannie had been struck dumb by her sadness. The only one who'd known what to say was Frederick. They'd grown closer and closer, until she couldn't fight it any longer. She'd decided – right here, at this very place – to break up with Harry and be with Frederick.

And then he'd left. Without a note; without saying goodbye. Just like her mother.

Jules's gut twisted. Even all these years later, she was haunted by the image of finding her mum lifeless in the bath of the hotel room she'd moved into after leaving Jules's father. There'd been no letter, no final call... nothing. Her father had shut down, refusing to talk about anything to do with her mother, and Jules had never been able to understand what might have gone wrong. She'd never understood what had gone wrong with Frederick either. The last time she'd seen him had been twenty years ago, here at the villa after her father treated them all to a final weekend together. Jules knew her dad had been trying to alleviate her grief, but it had only made it worse.

But things had turned out for the best, she told herself. After Frederick left, Harry had asked her to move in with him. And when she'd fallen pregnant unexpectedly with Ivy, he'd proposed, offering her the life she'd wanted. A life like her parents had had, with a solid marriage, big house and loving children – until it had all gone wrong. She'd grabbed the chance to have it again with both hands.

There'd been bumps along the way... bumps including the twins. The humiliation had been almost too much to bear, but Jules had gritted her teeth and carried on, trying her best to incorporate the girls into their life. No matter what mistakes her husband had made, she wouldn't be like her mother and abandon everything.

She didn't need to fear losers from the past. She was a mother and a wife now, not the vulnerable young woman shattered by grief that she'd been then. Anyway, Ellie had told her Frederick wasn't coming. Apparently, she'd managed to track him down as the owner of a guest house in Vietnam, but he hadn't even responded to her message. Relief had swept over Jules before she told herself not to be silly. He was the one who should be ashamed for taking off like that. She let out a huff.

'Gross, Jules. Did you snort?' Mia wrinkled her nose as they went inside the villa.

Jules bit back a response and followed them in. At least Frederick wouldn't be here to witness their terrible behaviour – and to clock their existence. He didn't need to know about any past mistakes.

God, this place, she thought, glancing around the foyer. Harry was right: it hadn't changed a bit. It was like stepping back in time... back to the night Frederick had taken her hand and propelled her up the stairs, and—

'We're coming down!' Ellie's voice floated from the winding stone staircase, and there was a clatter as she, Safet and Ahmed – filming everything, as usual – came into view.

Ellie looked good, Jules thought, taking in the dark hair that used to be mousy brown, the slender frame in a way more upscale dress than the usual New Look clothes Ellie had lived in, and the polished toenails. Even Harry was goggling at her as if he'd never seen her before, although Harry always goggled at anything with boobs. That had definitely never changed. It was a good thing Jules had never been the jealous kind; and, anyway, she knew Harry wouldn't leave her. He loved their life as much as she did.

'You're here!' Ellie's grin was massive. It was hard to harbour any negativity when someone looked at you like that. Ellie had always been so happy to be included as if she didn't deserve to occupy the space and was simply grateful to be there. It would have been annoying if she wasn't so nice. 'Hey, Nat and Mia.'

The girls nodded. 'I like your sandals,' Nat said, and Jules almost fell over. She couldn't remember the last time either of the twins had complimented her.

'Ivy not come?' Ellie padded down the stairs to give Jules a hug.

Jules cringed as Ellie touched the band of fat that ringed her waist, envy flooding in as her fingers grazed Ellie's spine through the thin fabric of her dress. She hadn't seen her spine in years, despite all her hard work at the gym. Granted, the wine hadn't really helped.

'Ivy had a party in the city she didn't want to miss.' Jules forced a smile and a shrug. 'Typical nineteen-year-old.' Hurt zinged through her as she remembered when she'd rung up her daughter to invite her along, hoping her presence would cushion the twins' aggression. Nat and Mia loved Ivy, hanging off her every word. And she'd barely seen her daughter these past few months. Jules missed her more than she ever could have imagined. Besides, she loved showing her off. Tall and willowy with wavy blonde hair like Jules's, Ivy wasn't only beautiful, she was *kind* too.

It hadn't been easy having a baby and settling down when, instead of getting her first job, she'd been researching colic. Or when Harry had been away for huge stretches of time for work, saying he was needed on-site. But she'd reminded herself this was her chance to get back the family she'd lost, and she'd made the best of it.

Thank God for Vannie, or she would have gone completely crazy. Vannie had always been there for her, right from the very first day of Uni. Jules hated to admit it, but after having almost everything taken care of by her parents at home, life in the austere student halls was a little daunting. Vannie was the expert on independent living, showing her how to make spag bol and clean the toilet in the en-suite. When Jules missed her parents, Vannie was always on hand to sit down and chat.

After Ivy's birth, Vannie had been the first to babysit whenever Jules needed a break. Even to this day, she didn't hesitate to whisk up the Northern Line with a bottle of her favourite champagne. Despite being the head of a busy advertising agency in Soho and having a carousel of girlfriends and boyfriends, she always made time. Jules had met Nicola, her latest, a few times now, and she was absolutely gorgeous. They should be here soon, actually. Jules had had to twist Vannie's arm to come, but she'd relented as always.

'Hi, Harry.' Ellie hugged Harry, then gave the twins a quick embrace. 'Why don't you guys go check out the annex?' she said. 'I think Victoria's in there somewhere.'

'Oh, there's an annex?' Jules asked. She couldn't remember anything like that before. 'The kids can sleep out there, then.' She smiled at Ahmed and his dark, watchful eyes, trying not to shy away from the phone he was holding up. He probably wasn't recording anything, and she realised it was a coping mechanism, but it was unnerving. 'You'd like that, right?' She turned to Ellie. 'And we can get some adult time to catch up without the kids underfoot.'

Ellie bit her lip as Ahmed clung to her, and Jules could see that she didn't want to let him go. But for God's sake, the child was eleven and he would only be a few metres away from the main house. It would be good for him to be with other kids.

'Give it a try,' Ellie said, stroking Ahmed's hair. 'If you don't like it, you can come back in and stay with me.'

Jules raised an eyebrow, wondering what Safet would think of that. Harry had kicked out Ivy after the first month, saying he needed to sleep and he needed his wife. She'd loved feeling so wanted, even as she hated being torn from her daughter. But Safet probably wouldn't mind. He was so calm, so gentle. She was dying to grab him for a quiet moment to themselves. Maybe they could even talk to Ellie this weekend, although perhaps this wasn't the place. She'd see what Safet thought.

'Vannie and Nicola should be here soon, and then I thought we could get started with drinks by the pool and make a plan for what we want to do the next few days.' Ellie's voice was confident, but her eyes were darting from Harry to Jules as if she was looking for approval. Jules's mind flashed back to Uni, when Ellie had wanted to put up a photo she'd bought in the shared kitchen. She'd looked exactly the same way. 'It's such a shame Frederick can't be here, and then we could have the whole gang.'

'Yes, a shame.' Jules made her smile brighter, even as her insides lurched once more at the name.

'Come on.' Harry put a hand on her back. 'Let's choose our room before Vannie comes and takes the best one, like always.'

Jules smiled, rolling her eyes. There'd always been a tension between those two, each one thinking they deserved more of her time and attention. But they usually limited it to sniping and sarcasm, and she'd learned to ignore it. On some level, she thought they might actually enjoy it. She followed her husband up the stairs, holding back the wave of memories threatening to engulf her. This was going to be good, she told herself. It was definitely worth making the journey here once more.

This weekend would be all about the future, not the past.

THREE
VANNIE

'I can't believe you didn't want to come. I mean, *look*. It's beautiful.' Nicola's face shone as she took in the stone villa in front of them.

Set in the middle of vineyards rolling away into the azure sky with sun streaming down, Vannie could see the attraction if you'd never been here before.

If you didn't have memories waiting to ambush you.

Memories of how lives had been damaged forever.

God, she hated this place. She hated what she'd done here; the lies she'd told – the lies she'd had to tell to protect the person she loved the most. Nicola was right: she hadn't wanted to come back. Not now, not ever. Hell, she hadn't wanted to come the first time.

She gritted her teeth as her girlfriend slammed out of the car. When Ellie had emailed the invite, she'd fired back a quick one-liner that she was swamped with work. Hanging out with all of them, so many years later, was just... well, why? She and Jules had stayed firm friends, of course. But while she'd been happy enough to share a house with Ellie and Safet in Uni – they were so quiet she hardly knew they were there half the time – a cursory glance at Ellie's yearly newsletter was all she needed or wanted to know about their life now. And Frederick... that was simply out of the question. Not that he would dare make an appearance, she reckoned. Not after what had happened. Not after all these years.

But like last time, Jules had begged her to come. And, as she'd expected, Frederick wouldn't be around, so here she was. Nicola had invited herself along, telling Vannie she'd been planning to book a last-minute getaway for them, anyway. Nicola was so impetuous it was believable, but Vannie knew the real reason: she wanted to run interference with Jules. Nicola tried to hide it, but Vannie could see how annoyed she was by Jules's constant presence in their lives. True, Vannie had cancelled dates at the last minute when Jules had needed something, or when Ivy, Jules's daughter, called with a crisis of the heart. But Jules and Ivy were family – the only family she'd ever had – and anyone who didn't understand that...

Vannie sighed, sitting in the hot car. Maybe it was time to ditch Nicola. Six months was a long time in her books, and although she'd enjoyed Nicola way more than any other recent relationship, she was never going to go the distance. There simply wasn't room in her life, and she didn't want to make any.

Too bad Ivy wasn't coming. Vannie would have loved to catch up with her. Usually, they met every week for coffee before Vannie started work, but Ivy had begged off lately, saying she was busy with Uni. Vannie missed their time together. She'd never had kids, and Ivy was like a daughter to her.

She slid from the car, trying to quell the emotions rising inside as the villa loomed over her. It was simply a building. Nothing more. No one but her knew the truth of what had happened here, and no one ever would. Her phone let off a volley of beeps, and she sighed. She really should be back in London. She'd never been able to resist Jules when she pulled that face with those big puppy-dog eyes.

She crunched across the gravel, remembering the day they'd met. They'd both been away from home for the first time, and Jules had turned up at the student halls with a doting mother and father, along with the contents of a small house. Vannie had come alone, her mum barely registering she was moving away. She'd lifted a hand to wave goodbye, not even bothering to get out of bed to see her only child off to Uni. Vannie wrinkled her nose, the stink of old cigarettes and stale sweat burned into her memory.

Her cheeks flushed as she thought how she hadn't even had a sheet to put over the terrible plastic cover on the mattress, and how Jules had given her one without her asking. Vannie had mumbled her thanks, in awe of the bubbly, beautiful girl who seemed so at ease despite being as new as the rest of them. But maybe it was easy to be like that when you'd always had parents to love and support you, Vannie had thought. Through her school years she'd watched other kids with their mums and dads, longing sweeping over her as they folded them into hugs or turned up at the school gate to collect them. She'd been lucky if her mother came home at night, and even though she'd learned from a young age to take care of herself, she didn't always want to. The emptiness echoed inside her, sometimes so loudly she could barely hear anything else. The only way to survive was to try not to let anyone see how sad she was.

Her friendship with Jules – and her parents – had changed all that. They'd swept her into their world and, for the first time, she felt cared for. They remembered her birthdays, made sure she wasn't alone during the holidays, and showed her a place where people loved and appreciated each other in a way she'd never experienced. She'd felt part of a family, and at last she could drop the awkward guard she'd had up for so long. It had been so easy to let herself fall into that place of comfort and love. Maybe too easy.

Then Jules's mother Anita had died, and everything changed. That had been almost as painful for Vannie as it had for Jules. For the first time, neither one of them could comfort the other. That was when Frederick had stepped in. Even though they'd shared accommodation for years, Frederick had seemed distant from their group. He was unfailingly polite and friendly, but he was always busy with his mates who were doing the same course as him. One night after Anita had passed, Jules had been in her room and unable to stop the sobs tearing at her throat. She couldn't breathe, she'd told Vannie, and for a second she'd thought she might die. Frederick had burst in and wrapped his arms around her, holding her until she'd calmed. Something changed between them then, and he became the one Jules turned to. When Jules had told Vannie that story later, it had broken her heart.

She forced her mind away from that horrible time.

'Hi, everyone! We're here!' Nicola's voice rang out in the vaulted entrance of the villa.

Vannie tried not to cringe. She was like an excited puppy. That's what she got for dating someone ten years younger, she thought.

'Hey! Finally!' Jules floated into the hall wearing a high-cut one-piece swimming costume with a sheer turquoise throw over it, managing to look elegant and casual at the same time. She really had no idea how beautiful she was, Vannie thought, constantly complaining about her weight and wrinkles. 'We've been waiting for you two for ages. Don't worry, though, we haven't got stuck into the wine yet.'

Vannie pulled her close, thankful Jules was still sober. She'd been worried about her drinking for a while now. She'd always drunk a lot, like Harry. But as the years went on, it seemed to be getting worse. Even Ivy had noticed.

'Hi, Nicola. Good to see you again.' Jules kissed Nicola on both cheeks, and Vannie winced as Nicola pulled away with a haughty expression. 'Grab a room to put your things in and then come down, OK? We'll all go out to eat later.'

'I've already booked a place.'

Ellie came into the room, and Vannie almost did a double take. It was true she hadn't seen her for years, but somehow the scrawny youth with mousy-brown hair had become this willowy woman with dark eyes, high cheekbones and long lashes to die for. Even Nicola was drooling. Vannie poked her in the ribs.

'Welcome, both!' Ellie hugged Vannie, then turned to Nicola. 'So happy to meet you! Was it you who convinced her to come?'

Nicola nodded, still eyeballing Ellie. If Vannie had been the jealous type, she wouldn't have been best pleased.

'Well, some of us can't drop everything and run off to France at any given moment,' Vannie said, the words flying out before she clocked what she was saying. If anything, Ellie was the one whose job was more important. It wasn't like Vannie's clients would die if she didn't complete some paperwork, but Ellie's might.

Ellie's cheeks coloured at Vannie's remark, but she didn't respond, and Vannie felt a flash of shame. She was better than that, and Ellie was hardly a threat. This place had unsettled her, but there was no reason to let it. The past was well and truly locked away.

'I'm so pleased we're all here now,' Ellie said. 'Come, put your things down and we can get this weekend started.'

They were about to turn away when they heard the crunch of tyres on the gravel as a car pulled up outside. Vannie looked at Ellie.

'Someone else coming?'

Ellie shook her head. 'No, everyone's here. I wonder who that is? Maybe the property manager forgot something.' She walked to the door and looked outside. 'Oh my God!' Her voice rose in a happy shriek.

Vannie covered her ears. Was there really a need to be *that* high-pitched? She and Jules followed Ellie outside, squinting into the sun to try to make out what on earth could stir such excitement.

As the familiar face came into focus, Vannie felt the darkness and fear she'd pushed down deep seep through her once more.

The past wasn't locked away. It was here.

And it had the power to change everything.

FOUR
JULES

'Frederick!' Ellie hurried across the gravel as Frederick got out of a taxi.

Jules swallowed, watching in disbelief. What the hell was he doing here? Hadn't Ellie said he'd never responded? She forced her smile bigger. It didn't matter whether he was here or not. In fact, she was glad he'd made it, after all. She would show him how wonderful her life had turned out without him. She put an arm around Harry, gratitude shooting through her when he tightened his grip on her too. Shame Ivy wasn't here, she thought, leaning into her husband. She would have loved to show off her daughter.

'Jesus fucking Christ,' Vannie was muttering beside her, her face twisted into a scowl. 'He's got some bloody nerve.' She reached out and grasped Jules's hand.

Jules squeezed back, thankful for the support even though she didn't need it. She drew in a breath as she remembered the last time she'd seen him. Well, maybe 'remembered' was the wrong word. Given how much she'd drunk that night, things were a blur. She and Harry had had a big fight – he'd thrown words at her that she didn't want to recall – and he'd stormed off, ducking into a taxi for Bordeaux. She'd grabbed a bottle of booze and drained half the contents, then dived into the pool, hoping to wash away the hurt and pain.

When she'd got out, the world had been hazy as the booze worked its magic. Frederick had been sitting there, waiting, to make sure she was OK. As she'd stared at him, the strength of her emotions overwhelmed her. He was the one who'd been there for her after her mum had died – not Harry, who'd escaped from her sadness by partying with his mates. He was the one who'd let her talk for hours without eyeing the mobile to see what messages he'd missed. And he was the one who'd talked of a future, inviting her to come to Asia with him after graduation.

Harry had told her he loved her, yes, but where had he been when she'd needed him? Wasn't real love staying beside you when times were tough? Wasn't that exactly what she wanted? She'd pulled Frederick close, and even though she was drunk and she knew she shouldn't be doing it, she'd kissed him. He froze, and for a second, she'd thought she'd made a mistake. Maybe he was simply being a friend. Maybe he didn't want her like she'd thought.

Then he'd tightened his grip on her and kissed her back, and the heady relief that had poured through her had almost knocked her off her feet. They'd gone up to the bedroom, and the rest was a blur.

She'd woken up alone, half-dressed under the bedcovers with a pounding headache, unsure exactly what had happened. The only thing she could recall was the happiness circling inside: the sense that things were right; that she might be able to escape her grief and the detritus of her present. Maybe she would go with him to Asia, like he'd asked. For the first time in ages, she was excited for the future.

She'd pulled on cut-offs and a T-shirt, splashed cold water on her face, and padded down the stairs, her face creasing in a smile as she smelled the strong coffee Frederick liked to make. She'd have a cup, and then she'd wake Harry from wherever he'd crashed and tell him they were no more. She didn't think he'd be surprised. She cringed, thinking she really should have done that before spending the night with Frederick. But then... after their fight and the words he'd thrown at her, how could Harry believe they stood a chance at staying together?

But it wasn't Frederick in the kitchen making his trademark coffee. It was Vannie, and what she'd said next had broken Jules's heart...

'I'm going to tell him to leave.' Vannie's voice jerked her back to the present, and Jules blinked. 'There's no way he can swan in here like nothing's happened.'

'No, don't.' Jules let out a breath, trying to slow her racing heart. 'That was years ago. And I want him to see that he didn't hurt me. That I'm... that I'm happy.' For some reason, the words stuck in her throat. But she was happy. She *was*. And soon, once she managed to get some time with Safet, she'd be even happier.

'Are you sure?' Vannie looked all too ready to tell Frederick to go, but Jules nodded. 'At least stay away from him,' Vannie said. 'You can be distant but cool.'

Jules nodded again. Distant but cool, she thought, even as she couldn't stop staring at him. His blonde hair was shot through with a silvery grey, making his blue eyes seem even bluer. His skin was tanned with wrinkles fanning out from his eyes, and he was as tall and slender as ever: the perfect combination of muscular and toned. Before she could stop herself, a memory flashed into her mind of his body pressed against hers, and her stomach lurched.

Actually, she *wouldn't* be distant or cool, she decided. She'd be friendly and warm, like she was to everyone. If she behaved any differently towards him, it would only show he still affected her.

'He's here!' Ellie was practically vibrating with excitement at having the whole group reunited. 'He never answered my message, but here he is!'

'Hope it's OK,' Frederick said in his low, warm voice.

Just hearing it sent shivers through Jules as if he was beside her again, telling her everything would be all right. She must have been an idiot to think he wanted a future with her.

'I wasn't going to make it, but then an opportunity arose in London that I couldn't pass up, and since this is on the way...' He smiled, his teeth white against the tan skin. 'I thought I would come and see how everyone is doing. It's been an absolute age.'

Jules kept the grin nailed to her face, despite the anger circling inside. If he'd really wanted to know, he could have looked them up on Facebook like the rest of the human race. 'It's good to see you,' she managed to say, hoping her voice seemed genuine.

'Yes, wonderful.' Vannie's voice sounded as if it was coming through gritted teeth.

Nicola was shooting them both puzzled glances. 'Hi, I'm Vannie's girlfriend, Nicola,' she said, leaning forward to kiss him on both cheeks. 'It's lovely to meet you.'

'You too,' Frederick said. 'Vannie, looking forward to catching up again.' Was Jules imagining it, or did his tone sound the opposite? But then Vannie *was* shooting daggers at him. 'And Jules—'

'It's great that you're here!' she trilled before he could finish. 'Can't wait to chat.' Never had she meant any words less. Being in the same room with him, smelling his scent, was making her want to throw up. He'd always used a cologne from his native Sweden, a heady concoction that made Jules think of pine needles, smoky air and scudding clouds. One whiff of it brought his presence so sharply into focus that one day when she'd been hurrying down Regent Street and smelled that scent, she'd frozen on the spot. Of course he hadn't been there.

Ellie put her arms around them all, seemingly oblivious to the tension. 'Come on, get settled in,' she said. 'Then why don't we change and head out for dinner? I've booked a really good place in the village.'

Probably the only place in the village, Jules thought, but she nodded and took advantage of the chance to slip away from Frederick.

'I'll tell the kids to get ready,' she called back, heading towards the annex. She was trembling and sweat had formed damp patches under her arms. If she couldn't keep it together, maybe she should keep her distance. Cool and calm was better than a nervous wreck.

'Girls!' She went into the annex, eyebrows rising at how the modern interior was so different from the traditional villa. It was like something from a design magazine.

No one responded, so she padded down the corridor to the lounge. The twins were showing Victoria something on their phones, all three of them laughing away. Ahmed was in the opposite corner, huddled into a ball as he angled his mobile towards her, then back towards the girls. Jules gave a quick shiver at the ever-present lens. She knew he meant no harm, but the twins were right: it was kind of creepy.

'Guys, we're going for supper now. Can you please get changed – maybe into the outfits I bought you?' Knowing the twins would likely be wearing ripped jeans held together by tiny threads and crop tops that had shrunk in the wash, she'd gone shopping and purchased them creamy tanks with blue denim capris. They'd look perfect in photos, posed against her blue ensemble and Harry's terracotta shirt. But the girls didn't even respond, and she imagined the outfits were probably crammed in the back of their wardrobes right now – if they'd even bothered to hang them up.

She gazed with envy at Victoria, who was wearing a halter-top jumpsuit with a cut that made her look graceful and slender. Her long dark hair was shiny and thick, unlike the feath-ered fuzz the twins sported. She'd offered so many times to take them shopping or to her hair salon. They'd laughed in her face, telling her they'd rather go bald than have hair like hers.

She sighed, reminding herself they had a difficult life with a mother whose only goal seemed to be to get as much money off Harry as possible. Funny how she hadn't realised that most of the money came from Jules.

'Be at the car in ten minutes, ready to go.' She wasn't sure if any of them had heard her, but she hadn't the energy to do her usual haranguing. She'd sic Harry on them if they didn't come. Annoyingly, the twins tended to do whatever he told them with little argument.

She tapped out a quick message to Safet, then wandered into the house. Even though she'd been trying so hard to stop drinking, she poured herself a large rosé to take the edge off, swallowed it down, then went up to her room. Quickly she pulled on a sky-blue dress that always gave her confidence, twisted her hair up into what she hoped was a chic topknot, and slicked on some lipstick. Not bad; it would have to do for now. Then she spritzed on some of her favourite perfume and hurried down the stairs.

'Ouf!' She knocked straight into someone and pulled back, laughing. 'I'm sorry, I—' Her words stopped when she saw who it was – smelled who it was – before she looked: that same piney, fresh scent as ever. 'Frederick.'

'Hey, Jules.' He took a step away from her as if he couldn't stand to be close. Well, the feeling was mutual. 'I know you said it was fine when the others were there, but I do hope it's OK that I've come?'

She swallowed, unable to answer. She wanted to say yes, but every bit of her felt the opposite. It was as if her body rejected his presence, and even though her head knew it shouldn't matter after so much time had passed, it did. It *did*.

She turned away and rushed down the stairs without answering, thinking the sooner she put some distance between them, the better. She could endure these few days, and when she got back to London, everything would be just as it was. Better, even.

She ducked into a car, closely followed by Vannie and Nicola, while Harry and the twins got in another one. A quick ten-minute ride down a leafy lane, and they were in the tiny village. Ellie ushered them through a restaurant and onto a large terrace at the back, overlooking the vineyards. The blue sky met pale orange and pinks as dusk fell. It was absolutely beautiful, but it didn't come close to making up for the horrific food, tasting overpoweringly of cooking oil and heavy cream. With the twins' constant whining, Ellie clutching onto Safet, and Frederick's gaze lasered upon her, the meal seemed endless.

Thank God for wine, she thought as she poured herself yet another glass, despite telling herself not to. She leaned against Harry as he tightened his arm around her shoulders, grateful once more for his solid presence. If only it could be like this between them all the time. But he was so busy, she told herself, and his job so consuming. No wonder he had little energy left over at the end of the day.

'This food is absolute shit.'

Mia's whiny voice pierced the bubble Jules had managed to pull around herself, and she sighed.

'Try to eat a bit or you'll be hungry,' she said, aware she was slurring her words, but beyond caring.

'I find that frequently exposing children to different foods helps,' Ellie said cheerfully. 'Victoria started eating sushi when she was two!'

'Maybe if they actually lived with me and not my husband's ex-mistress, I would.' The words slipped out before she could stop them, and she cringed as Frederick swung his gaze sharply towards her. The last thing she'd wanted was for him to know there'd been trouble with her and Harry.

She put a hand on Harry's arm to offset the words, even as anger bubbled inside. Who did Ellie think she was to offer parenting advice, of all things? If anyone needed advice, it was her, with how to get Ahmed off that phone filming everything. But the last thing she wanted was to deal with that hurt puppy-dog look all night. Safet had told her how sensitive she was, and she knew Ellie didn't mean anything by it. As usual, she was only trying to help. God knows she had enough on her plate.

'Sorry.' She touched Ellie's hand across the table.

The rest of the meal passed in relative peace, and finally it was time to head back to the villa. Jules could barely keep her eyes open now, let alone get back to the car.

'I'll help her,' she heard Vannie say as she felt Harry gently manoeuvring her to her feet. She swayed unsteadily, and Vannie held her up. 'Whoa there,' her best friend said. 'Go slowly, OK? How much have you had to drink?'

'Dunno.' Not enough to help cope with the feeling of Frederick's eyes on her every time she looked his way. 'Nat and Mia?'

'They've gone ahead with Harry,' Vannie said, slowly helping her through the restaurant and into the car. Nicola grabbed their handbags and followed behind, then opened the car door and started the engine.

'I'll drive,' she said, 'seeing as how I'm the only one who hasn't consumed more than a bottle of wine.' Her tone was so annoyed that even Jules, as drunk as she was, couldn't ignore it.

Jules's stomach just about managed to stay put through the twists and turns of the narrow lane back to the villa, but she was green by the time they pulled up in front of the house. 'Oh, God,' she moaned. 'Why did I drink that much? Why?'

She noticed Nicola meeting Vannie's eyes over the top of her head as she got out of the car. 'Why *did* you drink that much?' Nicola muttered, and Vannie shot her a look.

'I'll help you to bed,' Vannie said, taking her arm once more.

'Maybe Harry can?' Nicola's voice was sharp. 'He is her husband, after all.'

'I'm here now.' Vannie's voice was as sharp. 'You go have a drink by the pool. I'll be there in a bit.'

Nicola stalked off, her lips in a tight line.

'She doesn't look very happy,' Jules commented, much louder than she'd meant to.

'She'll be fine.' Vannie manoeuvred Jules up a step. 'Now come on, let's get you sorted out.'

Jules let herself be guided by Vannie onto the bed, easing down under the covers. It was so nice to let someone take care of her, for once. For a minute, it felt like all the years between them had vanished – as if they'd gone back in time, twenty years earlier. The voices drifting up from the pool; the music; even the way her head was spinning. His arms around her, his mouth on hers...

'Do you remember that night?' The words trickled out as Vannie tucked the pillow under her head.

'What night?' Vannie's voice sounded so, so far away.

Jules opened her mouth to say more, but her eyes closed and sleep slipped over her.

FIVE

ELLIE

Ellie rinsed the dirty wine glasses in the kitchen, trying not to feel disappointed. It was ridiculous that she *would* feel disappointed, given she was in a beautiful villa in France with her husband, two kids and their friends. It was just... She turned off the water and leaned against the counter. This first night, she'd envisioned them all having a wonderful meal, then coming home and sitting round the pool with drinks, reliving old times while the kids cavorted in the water.

Instead, the meal at the place she'd chosen had been a disaster, with terrible food and non-existent service, and the mood around the table had been as dire as the food. Jules had bitten her head off when she dared offer some support, then got wasted. Vannie had spent the whole time keeping an eye on Jules, while Nicola's face got darker and darker. Safet had sat there silently checking his phone, while Frederick simply stared at Jules the whole time.

The only one who seemed to have any fun at all was Harry, who couldn't keep his hands off his wife. She got it, Ellie thought, hating the bitterness inside. They were in love. They had a great marriage. They didn't have to rub everyone's face in it. She sighed and put away the last glass before sitting down on a bar stool. She didn't need to be bitter. She had a great marriage too. But *she* had wanted to be the loved-up one at the table, and Safet had seemed a million miles away. He'd be OK once the adoption was sorted. She would, as well.

She closed her eyes, remembering the day Safet had come home from the refugee charity they both worked for. He'd told her that one of his outreach workers had found a young boy camping in the bushes at the side of a motorway where he'd fled from the lorry he'd travelled to England in. Her heart had broken at the thought, and she'd agreed without hesitation when Safet asked if the boy could stay with them until a foster family was found.

Days had stretched into weeks, and soon, the idea of Ahmed leaving was unbearable. With his family killed by fighting in Syria, he'd agreed to let them adopt him. For Safet, it was like being able to reach back in time to give himself exactly what he'd wanted after losing his family in the Bosnian war. He'd been only a couple of years older than Ahmed when he'd made his way to England all alone too.

'Any of that red left?' Nicola appeared beside her, rooting through the cupboard where Ellie had shoved all the wine she'd bought after a quick trip to the local supermarket.

'Plenty.' Ellie smiled and handed over a bottle. 'Here. Pour me a glass too, will you?' She rarely drank and she'd already had a glass at supper, but Jules's sharp remark and her upset over how things had unfolded today made her want to dim her nerves.

'With pleasure.' Nicola deftly opened the bottle with a corkscrew, poured them both a liberal glass, then took a swig. 'Christ, this is foul.'

Ellie managed to keep her face neutral as she took a sip of her drink, irritation stirring inside. What was it with these people? Everything she did seemed wrong. She'd spent half an hour inside the terrible supermarket trying to make sure the wines she chose wouldn't offend anyone's sensibilities. Anyway, it wasn't foul. She loved the peppery taste on her tongue. She took another sip.

'Vannie still upstairs with Jules?' It was a stupid question, but she had nothing to say to Nicola, now perched on a stool beside her. At least someone wanted to talk to her, she thought.

'Yup. I think Jules was a little worse for wear,' Nicola said, rolling her eyes. 'Putting it mildly. And of course Vannie would do anything for her friend.'

'Well, they have been friends for a very long time,' Ellie said. They'd always been thick as thieves, ever since they'd met. Vannie had even gone to Jules's place for Christmas that first year, and then every holiday after. At first, Ellie had desperately wanted to break into their tight twosome, envious of their laughter drifting out from the communal kitchen every night. But whenever she joined them, she could never muster up anything interesting to say, and they didn't even seem to notice when she left. She'd always found making friends difficult, perhaps because she couldn't believe anyone would *want* to spend time with her. The ease with which she and Safet had connected seemed nothing short of miraculous.

Nicola ran a finger around the rim of her glass. 'Vannie does way too much for her, in my opinion. We can barely get through a meal together without her texting Jules or Ivy, for God's sake. I get that they're old friends, but it might be time to let go a bit. If I wanted a threesome, I would have asked.'

Ellie drew back, surprised at the words. She'd never met anyone who didn't like Jules. Everyone was drawn to her. But then it might be a bit different if you had to watch your partner unable to resist that flame.

'Are you good friends with Jules, then?' Nicola asked, downing her drink and pouring another. Ellie couldn't help thinking that, for something Nicola had deemed foul, she seemed to be getting through the wine rather quickly. 'I never heard Vannie mention you before you started organising this weekend.'

Ellie felt the old familiar hurt go through her, but she pushed it away. Why would Vannie mention her? Their lives rarely intersected now. 'We've kept in touch on and off over the years, like old friends do,' she mumbled, ignoring the fact that it was mostly her who sent emails. 'Jules has done a few fundraising events with us.'

'Oh, I'm surprised.' She wiped her mouth. 'Your husband certainly seems to know her well.'

Ellie raised her eyebrows. What was Nicola on about? Even when they'd seen Jules those rare times over the years, Safet had only spoken to her briefly. 'What do you mean?'

'Well, he definitely texts her a lot.'

Ellie's mouth dropped open. What? Safet texting Jules? She shook her head to clear it, wishing she hadn't had that extra drink. Maybe she hadn't heard right. That must be it. Safet didn't even know Jules's number. Why would he be texting her?

'No, you must be wrong.' Ellie could hardly get the words out.

Nicola tilted her head. 'I saw it myself. Jules left her phone on the table at supper. When I picked it up, there were quite a few notifications for texts from him. I couldn't see what they said, but I did think it was odd that they were texting when they're staying in the same house. I mean, why not just talk to each other? Unless you have something to hide, of course.' She looked like she was enjoying this.

Ellie stared, her mind racing. Something to hide? Not Safet. He was the most open, honest man she ever could have asked for. He had never hidden anything from her... not even some of the things he'd done to survive; things she hadn't really wanted to hear. He'd been determined to tell her, saying if she wanted to know the best of him, she had to know the worst of him too.

Love swelled inside as she remembered that first walk they'd taken together while the party raged on in the student halls. Neither one of them had wanted to be in the midst of downing shots and blaring music, so they'd wandered into the soft September night, following the winding paths that took them through fields away from the sprawl of the Uni. She'd told him all about growing up in a small town outside London, with her mum and dad and older sister who'd been the best at everything. She said how she'd never felt noticed – that no matter how hard she'd tried, her sister had got there first and done it better.

And then Safet had told her his story, and never had she felt more embarrassed for daring to complain about her childhood. He'd told her how not only his family but his village had been practically wiped out. How he'd had to sleep in the forest, stealing food from wherever he could. How he'd been attacked one night on the street and what, in a fit of rage, fear and despair, he'd done to the man who'd tried to hurt him. How he'd piled into the back of a lorry and got into Britain, fearful he might die. How he'd made it, but then faced years of struggle to build a life there.

She'd put her arms around him, and he'd gripped her as if he never wanted to let go. Awe and admiration filled her that he'd been through so much and yet still managed to make it to university, in a country not his own, in a language he'd conquered only a few years earlier. She became his family and he hers, even though her parents were only miles away. The bond between them was strong from the very start, growing from friendship to love and becoming ever stronger with their own family. Safet would never do anything to threaten that.

But then... Ellie sipped her wine. He had been acting strangely lately, that was true. Twitchy, staring at his phone more than usual, like he had over supper. She'd put it down to the adoption, but what if it was more? If what Nicola saw was right, then he *had* been messaging Jules – or at least Jules had been messaging him. But there had to be an explanation. Whatever the reason he was texting Jules, he wouldn't betray her. She trusted him. She knew how important family was to him and how he'd do anything for them. There was no need to even give it a second thought.

And now, she had to stop drinking.

'Right.' She feigned a yawn. 'I'm going to hit the sack.'

'Already?' Nicola looked horrified. 'It's only ten o'clock!'

Ellie shrugged. 'I'm exhausted.' The evening had seemed endless, and she was ready to put it all to bed now. Safet was a night owl, so she could rely on him to check in on Victoria and make sure Ahmed stayed fast asleep. She bit her lip, thinking of her son in the annex. He hadn't wanted to come here, remembering France as the place where he'd slept in a cold tent for weeks, hungry and tired. Safet had to explain *this* France was different, but he'd stayed anxious and nervy. He'd spent the whole meal glued to her side, staring at his mobile and then grabbing Safet's when his battery ran out.

But Safet would be up for ages yet if Ahmed needed them. He was the only one who could calm him down, anyway. Oddly, even though Ahmed had no clue what Safet was murmuring in his soft melodic Bosnian, the cadence would relax him so much he'd often fall asleep in Safet's arms.

Tomorrow was a new day. Everyone would settle in tonight, and by morning they'd be laughing and trading memories, looking back with awe at how far they'd all come.

She'd been right to bring them here again. Soon, they'd see that too.

SIX
JULES

Jules awakened the next morning with a jolt, a sharp pain crashing through her head. She groaned, grabbing the glass of water someone – Vannie? – had thoughtfully left by the side of the bed. Beside her, Harry lay on his back with his mouth wide open, snoring so loudly she could almost feel her bones rattle. She usually rammed in earplugs back at home, but she'd passed out last night before he'd come to bed.

She sat up now, groaning. Why oh why had she drunk so much? Then she remembered. *Frederick.* Frederick was here. He'd been staring at her over supper, his eyes silently evaluating who she was now; what she had become. So she'd done what she always did when she was feeling uncomfortable: she drank. She knew she had to stop. It had been getting worse over the years, and a forty-one-year-old drunk was much less acceptable than a twenty-one-year-old one. She had started cutting down when she'd got in touch with Safet, and she'd been doing so well these past few weeks until last night.

She rolled out of bed and into the en-suite bathroom, trying not to disturb Harry. Not that he'd wake up, anyway: when Ivy was a baby and Jules was half-dead with exhaustion, she'd try to get him to take a turn when Ivy cried at night. But he'd sleep through the cries and her frantic prods until she'd give up and go to the baby herself. The funny thing was that one ding from his WhatsApp jerked him awake instantly now. Shame Whats-App hadn't been around when Ivy was young, or Jules would have set it as his alarm.

After a cold shower and two ibuprofen, she started to feel human again. Twisting her wet hair into a bun, she threw on a pair of cut-off jean shorts and her favourite soft T-shirt. No one would be awake at this hour, and she was hoping to do some yoga by the pool. The light would be perfect to take some photos for her socials.

The house was quiet as she padded down the stairs and out to the pool area. She stood for a minute, basking in the early-morning sun, breathing in that salty scent of the vineyards. Then she stretched her arms up, feeling the muscles lengthen and hum.

'Good morning.'

'Oh!' She turned towards the voice, startled to see Frederick on a lounger on the opposite side of the pool. Her pulse started racing, and she drew in a breath. *Calm down*, she told herself. 'I didn't see you there.' She ran a hand over her wet hair, thinking she must look a state. 'What are you doing up so early?'

'Jet lag,' Frederick responded, grimacing. 'My body is all over the place.'

Jules nodded, unable to stop herself eyeing him at the mention of his body. His long legs were stretched out in front of him on the lounger, as toned as they had been in his twenties. He'd filled out a bit since he was young, but not in the thick meaty way most men his age had. She tore her gaze from him, conscious she was staring. Cool and distant, she reminded herself. After what he'd done, this man didn't deserve anything from her.

'How are you feeling this morning?' he asked.

Jules's cheeks flushed at how drunk she'd got. God, she must have made a spectacle of herself. *Damn* him for coming!

'Vannie helped you to bed, right? So you and Vannie are still close?' Frederick's tone was careful. But what did he care? Why was he asking about Vannie?

'Yes, we're still friends,' she said. 'Good friends.' She'd almost said best friends, but it sounded so juvenile in a forty-one-year-old. It was true, though. They'd been through so much together, bonded by the good times and the bad.

She'd never forget Vannie's face the day they'd met: the longing as she stared at Jules and her parents, quickly replaced by a bright smile and firm handshake. Jules had had to hide her grin. What eighteen-year-old shook hands with her flatmate? But there was something endearing about Vannie's forthrightness, and Jules loved the way Vannie's eyes tracked her as if she was under a spotlight. Jules's parents treated her the same way at home: the star in their show. Jules's family had returned the attention to Vannie in spades, practically adopting her. Vannie had lapped it up, and Jules had loved having someone who felt like a sister. When Jules's mother died, Vannie had been almost as devastated as Jules had been. Jules understood, though. Her mother had been like a mum to Vannie too. Her friend had been so engulfed by her grief that Jules had turned to Frederick for support.

She dropped her head, once more remembering the day she discovered her mother's body. Jules had called 999 in a panic, then rung Vannie. She couldn't recall what she'd said. All she knew was that Vannie was beside her in what felt like minutes, her face pale and body shaking as they clutched each other's hands while her mother was wheeled out.

At every key moment in her life, Jules thought, Vannie had been there – even when she didn't agree with Jules's decisions, the mark of a true friend. It was odd to think of now, but Vannie hadn't wanted her to have Ivy, even going as far as saying she could take Jules to a clinic if she wanted a termination. And when Harry had proposed, Vannie had tried to put her off, asking over and over if this was what she really wanted. Jules knew that Vannie had never been Harry's biggest fan, but that had been like a slap in the face.

But everything had worked out. Ivy had only brought them closer in the end. Vannie had stepped up to support her, and Jules couldn't have asked for a better godmother to her child. She watched out for Ivy the same way she watched out for Jules. If there was anyone she trusted with her daughter – with her life – it was Vannie.

'Jules, I'd really like to talk to you, if that's OK.' Frederick was looking at her with hopeful eyes.

'I've got nothing to say to you.' The words escaped in a croak, and she made a big show out of clearing her throat. 'Think I'll head into the village and pick up some fresh croissants,' she mumbled, even though Ellie had stocked the place with enough food and alcohol to last them a month.

'Maybe I can come with you – we can get away from here for a bit?' Frederick asked, getting up and coming towards her. 'If you're comfortable with that, of course.'

No. No *way*. She blinked as a memory flooded into her head – a memory of a day like this one, the first morning at the villa then too. She and Frederick had been the only ones awake, and they'd been dying for some croissants. There'd been a few rickety old bicycles around, and Frederick had dared Jules to race him to the village.

She'd been in great shape from all her Pilates, her arms toned and her legs stronger than ever. She'd jumped on the bike and they'd started pedalling, laughing as they flew down the lane together with the rusty bike chains rattling. The soft June air on her arms; the sun slanting through the leafy trees above them; Frederick's blue eyes smiling over at her, full of admiration... she'd felt a moment of such pure happiness, tears came to her eyes.

They'd raced into the village neck and neck, with Jules pulling into the lead as the bakery came into view. She suspected Frederick had let her win, but she wasn't going to look a gift horse in the mouth: winning was winning. She got off the bicycle, cheeks flushed and hair curled around her face, and grinned.

'Loser buys the croissants.' She laughed as Frederick smiled good-naturedly and went inside the small shop. Harry would have argued for hours why he shouldn't have to buy them, she'd thought to herself. Hell, he never would have let her win in the first place – if indeed that's what Frederick had done. Harry might love her, but he always aimed for the top. She admired that about him, but after what she'd been through, it was nice to know someone had her back.

'That's all right,' she said now, forcing a grin. 'I don't mind going to get them. You relax here.'

But Frederick didn't move away. His face was serious, and his eyes pierced into her. 'Look.' He sighed. 'I can see you're not thrilled to have me here. I don't blame you, given... given the past. I don't need to stay, but I do need to talk. You're the reason I came in the first place.'

She was the reason he'd come in the first place? Anger shot through her. Whatever he wanted to say, he was twenty years too late. Quite frankly it was a little pathetic that he wanted to talk to her so much he'd travelled all this way. It was too late to change anything.

'I don't want to talk to you,' she said, struggling to keep her voice even. 'There's no reason. It's all in the past.'

But Frederick was shaking his head. 'That's just it, Jules. There's something I...' He swallowed. 'Something I found out. It's not in the past. You know it's not. And we need to talk. Please. We—'

'Hey, party people!' Vannie's voice interrupted them, and Frederick swore under his breath. 'How are you feeling?' She put an arm around Jules, and Jules thought she'd never been so happy to see her friend. Thank God for Vannie.

'I'm great, actually.' Her voice had a hint of defiance to it. 'I'm about to go get some croissants. I'll catch you all later.'

Jules hurried to her room to grab her keys and wallet, then went out to the car. Whatever Frederick was so keen to talk to her about, he could keep it to himself. She wasn't interested; not one bit. She had a life now, and she didn't need any apologies or excuses – or any reminders of what could have been.

And actually... Determination shot through her. When she got back to the villa, she'd tell him she didn't want him here. She'd ask him to go. He'd be leaving once more, but this time, she'd be the one calling the shots.

SEVEN

VANNIE

Vannie vibrated with tension as she sat by the pool, barely taking in the kids dive-bombing around her or Ahmed filming the action with his phone. All she could think about was Frederick. Frederick, and Jules. What the *hell* was he doing here? Why had he come back after all this time? Had he known Jules would be here? Had he come to apologise?

How much did he actually remember about that night? She'd tried to prise some answers out of him after everyone had gone to bed, but he'd walked off, saying he wasn't going to waste his time with her until he'd spoken to Jules. She'd barely been able to sleep all night.

She let out a huff, and Nicola glanced over. Anger and irritation poured through Vannie as she met her girlfriend's eyes. She'd wanted to get up early this morning and have a second to clear her head – and, most of all, try to think of a plan to ensure Jules and Frederick kept away from each other. Instead, she'd spent ages lying in bed listening to Nicola whine about how much time she'd spent with Jules last night, and how she hadn't come here to play third wheel. And when she'd managed to get out of the bedroom, Jules and Frederick had been chatting by the pool.

And then Jules had taken off.

What had he said?

She gazed over at Harry. He'd seemed as annoyed as her when Frederick had turned up. He'd been more affectionate with Jules last night than Vannie had seen in ages. He'd been concerned, too, when he couldn't find Jules this morning – a departure from his usual blasé behaviour towards his wife. From what Vannie had noticed over the years, he came home late, gave Jules a quick kiss on the cheek before heading to what Jules called his 'man cave' in the basement they'd had dug at an exorbitant price. Jules would roll her eyes and joke that she was lucky if he even grunted in her direction. Sometimes, Vannie wondered how that could be enough for her friend, but she did have Ivy to plug any gaps in her life – and Vannie, of course. Despite the drinking, she seemed happy enough, thank God. Vannie couldn't bear to think of her being sad, especially after all she'd been through with her mother's death. Her life had been perfect until then, and the grief had almost destroyed her. Perhaps that was why she seemed content to stay in her marriage: nothing could ever be as bad as losing her mum.

Was Harry nervous because Frederick was here? After all these years, was he worried the attraction between them lingered? Surely not. But fear needled inside, and Vannie bit her lip, remembering what his worry had propelled him to ask her all those years ago.

Ask, then threaten.

It had been the last term at Uni, a few weeks before the end. They'd all been sharing a house close to campus, the same one since leaving halls after their first year. Ellie was already lamenting having to leave, but Vannie couldn't wait to get out of there. Living together had seemed the easiest thing to do after their first year ended, but as time had gone on, she'd grown more and more annoyed by Harry's blokey behaviour – and had even less to say to Ellie and Safet. Frederick was the only one besides Jules that she really respected, but he was usually so busy studying for his engineering degree that he rarely went out with them. And after Jules's mum had died in January, the last few months had been such a shit show that Vannie was desperate for a fresh start, somewhere not tainted by sadness and grief.

Vannie had been in her room revising for finals while Jules and Frederick chatted in the lounge. They'd been spending a lot of time together, and Vannie wondered if Harry had noticed them edging closer and closer. He was like a kid in a way: unsure what to do when things weren't happy and fun; unable to adapt when the situation required. And Jules had never needed anything from him... until now.

Her laugh had floated through the house, and Vannie felt something inside her lift. That had been the first time she'd heard her friend laugh in months. Guilt had flooded in that she hadn't been able to give Jules the support she'd needed after finding her mother's body. She would never be able to forgive herself, and every time she saw Jules's pain her gut clenched and she'd have to retreat to the bathroom to take deep breaths until the nausea subsided.

She'd heard someone come into her room, and she'd glanced up to see Harry.

'I need a favour,' he'd said, and Vannie had raised her eyebrows. That was a first. He was more likely to mock her than ask for help. Sometimes, she wondered how Jules put up with him, but he was a different person with her... like the man he thought she wanted: posh, confident, clever.

Vannie wasn't sure if Jules knew that wasn't the real Harry. Sure, the private-school bursary had allowed him to acquire an air of class, but despite the rounded vowels he'd come from an estate on the outskirts of Manchester, much like the one she'd grown up on. She'd met his mum the one time she'd showed up to drop Harry off, after Christmas their first year. Surprised by the bleached-blonde hair and strong Mancunian accent, Vannie had paused to chat to her. She'd never seen Harry more livid; as soon as he spotted them lingering outside the student halls, he'd marched his mum away – and he'd been awful to Vannie ever since.

She got it, though. Vannie reminded him of their shared beginnings: a battered estate, single parent, dragging themselves up through sheer will. They'd both tried to distance themselves from the past as much as possible. Jules, with her confidence and gloss, represented a different world – one of ease and affection. Vannie wasn't even sure Jules knew where Harry had come from, or if she'd met his mother. She had simply accepted him into her life, as she had Vannie, uninterested in anything that existed outside her orbit.

'What do you want?' Vannie had said, expecting him to ask to borrow money. No matter how much Jules gave him, he never seemed to have enough.

'I need your help to keep Jules away from Frederick when we go to France,' he'd said.

Vannie snorted. So he had noticed! She'd wondered how long it would take him, but it was none of her business.

'Please.'

'I'm not the love police, Harry.' Instantly she regretted using the word 'love' as Harry's face darkened even more.

'No, but you're her best friend,' he said. 'And she trusts you. So... maybe, talk to her? Make sure she knows how much I love her?' Harry actually looked worried. Maybe it had finally hit him how shit he'd been, and how wonderful Frederick was. 'I know I haven't been the best boyfriend lately, but I really want to make it up to her – and I have something important to ask her.'

Vannie had stared, trying to read him. Did Harry really love

Jules? They had a lot of fun – or they had, before her mum died. They looked great together, too, and Jules was incredibly generous with him, giving him whatever he wanted. Like Vannie, Harry had never had that before. Maybe for Harry, that *was* love. But Vannie wasn't sure that version of love was enough to keep them together. From what she'd seen, Jules and Frederick had a genuine connection. Frederick was warm and solid, and she knew he cared about Jules. And Jules was herself with him, the beautiful, kind woman Vannie loved, not the golden-girl she portrayed when she was with Harry. Vannie would do anything to help bring happiness back to her friend, and if that meant being with Frederick, then she wasn't going to stand in their way. If anything, she would encourage it.

But when she'd said as much to Harry, he hadn't been best pleased... putting it mildly. His face had hardened, and he'd stormed from the room. She'd thought that would be the end of it, but she couldn't have been more wrong. If only he hadn't found what she'd been so desperate to hide, then he wouldn't have returned to ask even more of her.

If only she hadn't agreed.

'I come bearing croissants!' Jules swept into the pool area, her arms full of bags from the bakery. 'Here, have one.' She dropped a pastry onto Vannie's lap.

Vannie stared hard at her. There was no way she'd look as cheery as this if Frederick had spoken to her about their last night here. Thank God. Thank *God*.

The children streaked from the pool, the twins reaching Jules first and practically knocking her over in their haste to get the best pains au chocolat. Vannie shook her head as she watched them. They were their father's daughters, that was for sure. Or maybe their mother's, since all Vannie heard about the woman was how much money she wanted.

As for Ivy, well... Ivy was a different story. Vannie smiled as she thought of her god-daughter. Jules had been so young when she'd had her, and without a mother to lean on, it was Vannie she'd called when she needed a hand or when she was desperate to sleep. Harry had been travelling so much with work that he hadn't been there, and Vannie had been only too happy to muck in and help.

Her heart softened as she remembered giving Ivy her bottle in a darkened room, the baby's huge blue eyes looking up at her as if she could see right into her soul. Ivy had drifted off to sleep, a warm solid weight in Vannie's arms, and Vannie had sat there for hours, not wanting to move even if she could. Ivy had been the first baby that made her think she might actually want children one day, and they'd stayed close all these years. She was the one Ivy called when she wanted advice about relationships and men, even though she knew Vannie really didn't have a clue about men – or women, for that matter.

'I can't believe Jules bought all those croissants. I'd just started laying out a big continental buffet.' Ellie appeared at her side, her face creased into a frown, looking so much like the girl who'd caught them smoking in Jules's bedroom. Vannie had sighed when she'd seen her come in – she'd known Ellie was going to be a stickler, the one who would spoil everything, and their little unit had been so good until now – but Ellie's desire to join in eclipsed her rule-following nature. She'd taken the cigarette they'd offered her and sat down beside them, although Vannie didn't think she'd ever actually smoked it.

'Be happy you don't have to do that now,' Vannie said. 'Sit down, relax.' She gestured to the chair next to her, but Ellie turned and grabbed a pastry for Ahmed before the girls devoured them all. Vannie sighed. How was that boy ever going to learn to make his way in this strange world if Ellie didn't let him?

'Funny that Frederick showed up.' Harry's voice floated over, and Vannie jerked. 'I thought he'd forgotten all about us.'

Vannie swivelled to meet Harry's eyes. 'Yes. Funny.' God, she wished it was funny. And that he'd forgotten.

Harry stared at her, and Vannie flinched at the calculating look. Suddenly, that same flash of fear went through her, growing bigger in the silence. Frederick hadn't said anything, had he? Was he about to ruin everything?

'I need your help,' Harry said.

Vannie's heart dropped. No. Not again. What could he want this time?

'Look, Harry, if this is about Frederick, then you have nothing to worry about,' she said. 'Jules is going to stay well away from him. She doesn't even want to talk to him.' Thank God.

Harry laughed. 'No, no, I couldn't care less about him. Jules and I have been together for twenty years. If that isn't a solid marriage, then what is?' His eyes bore into her, and she flinched. How would she know what a solid marriage was? Her longest relationship had been... she cringed, trying not to think of it.

'Well, what do you want me to do?' she asked, more out of curiosity than a desire to help.

'This is an important weekend. I need to discuss something with Jules, and I need her to be in a good mood when I do.'

Vannie swallowed, thinking how much this conversation mirrored the one from years ago. Foreboding swept over her. 'I might be able to control a lot, but that doesn't extend to your wife's moods.'

'Keep her sober, OK? She must have had three bottles yesterday. She couldn't even stand, let alone have a conversation.'

Vannie looked pointedly at the glass in his hand, and he snorted. 'It's just a little drink to get me going. I'm hardly drunk. But if she keeps going like last night, then I'll never get the chance to talk to her.'

'What do you need to talk to her about?' She knew it was

none of her business, but she couldn't help wondering. Jules hadn't said a word about any trouble between them. But then, Jules never talked about Harry, shutting down any questions Vannie asked. And although Harry had fucked up on a major scale with the twins, Vannie did have to admit he'd seemingly reformed his ways. He might not be present emotionally, but at least he hadn't strayed again.

'None of your business, Vannie.' Harry held her gaze. 'Nothing for you to be worried about. Not this time, anyway.'

Vannie blinked, then cursed to herself. She didn't want to show how much she still thought about what he knew about her and how it could blow everything apart. 'I'll try to stop her drinking so much,' she said through gritted teeth.

'Good.' Harry leaned back, looking at her smugly. 'Now, let's enjoy the weekend, shall we?'

Fat chance of that, Vannie thought. She couldn't wait until it was over.

EIGHT

ELLIE

Ellie wiped another plate and put it on the sideboard. How was it that she always ended up in the kitchen, tidying up after everyone? Her mind flashed back to the kitchen in the house-share. She'd done load after load of dishes there, too, often with Safet by her side helping. And no one ever said thank you, or even seemed to notice they'd been done. Why didn't she say no?

She sighed, gazing at the untouched food on the table. She'd started setting out an amazing buffet with fruit, yoghurt and every kind of cereal imaginable, but after Jules had burst in carrying practically a whole bakery's worth of pastries, no one had wanted to touch her offerings. They'd swarmed around the pool, stuffing their faces, and by the time she'd managed to get out there, it had all been gone except for the one she'd saved for Ahmed.

She took a deep breath, telling herself to calm down. This wasn't the real reason she was so on edge. It was Safet... and Jules. What was going on? The more she told herself it was silly and he could never do that to her, the more she longed to hear him say those words. She'd wanted to ask him this morning, but he'd slipped out while she was sleeping. He'd left a note saying he'd gone for a walk.

'Ellie, can I have a glass of water?' Out of nowhere, Mia appeared at her side, closely followed by Nat.

Ellie blinked at their heavily made-up faces slathered in foundation. Foundation! As if they needed that at their age with their perfect skin. Victoria had begged for a product that had gone viral on TikTok, but Ellie had flat out refused, saying she was too young and—

Oh, God. She gulped as Victoria appeared behind the twins, her face made up exactly like theirs with lashings of heavy black mascara and thick pencilled-in eyebrows. She met Ellie's eyes defiantly as if she was daring her mother to make a comment. Ellie bit back the remark that was waiting to come out, trying to arrange her face into a neutral expression.

'Of course you can have some water,' she said, congratulating herself on the fact that her voice sounded normal and not horrified. 'The glasses are up there. The water's lovely and cold.' She flipped on the tap to get it running, but the twins looked disgusted.

'We're not drinking that,' Nat said as if she'd offered them poison. 'We only have bottled water.'

Ellie raised an eyebrow. They never had bottled water at home, and if she ever dared to buy any, Victoria would berate her for not caring about the environment. She waited for her daughter to say something, but Victoria wouldn't meet her eyes.

'Well, you can check the fridge, then,' she said, watching as they ransacked the contents without even saying thank you – or offering a bottle to Victoria.

They cracked their bottles open and took a drink, then nudged Victoria. 'Can you ask her now?' Nat said.

Victoria nodded. 'Mum, does Ahmed have to stay in the annex with us?' She pushed her hair behind her ear.

Ellie stared, trying to get a grip on how different her

daughter looked with all that make-up. It was like she'd morphed into someone else.

'What do you mean?' Ellie asked. 'He's your brother. It would be nice for him to be with you and not feel left out.'

'But...' Victoria wound a strand of hair around her finger, pulling it tighter and tighter.

Ellie watched as the tip of her finger went red. 'What?'

'He's always filming us,' Mia said, before Victoria could continue. 'And TBH, Ellie, it's bang out of order for you to let him perv around us like that.'

Her voice was so supercilious that, for a second, Ellie couldn't believe it had come from a child more than half her age. She tried to clamp down on the anger circling inside. *Perv around?* Ahmed was only eleven, for God's sake.

'It's his way of dealing with everything,' Ellie said, attempting to keep her voice level. 'I'm sure Victoria told you about his background.' She tried to meet her daughter's eyes, but she refused to look at her. She sighed, thinking that maybe she should have a word with Ahmed and ask him to cool it with the mobile around the girls. Teens that age were so self-conscious; it was no wonder they didn't want to be filmed all the time. Victoria wouldn't even let her keep a photo on her phone unless she approved it.

'Please, Mum,' Victoria said. 'He's so annoying. I *hate* having him at home all the time. Can't you let me get away from him here?'

Ellie jerked in surprise. She knew having Ahmed around was an adjustment, but she'd never heard her daughter sound like this... so angry. A noise came from outside the door, and they all turned to see Ahmed hovering by the entrance. Oh, *shit*. Her heart dropped as she took in his brown, soulful eyes and the sadness on his face. How much had he heard?

'Ahmed, I—' But before she could finish, he took off, ducking and twisting away from her.

She let out a breath and turned to face Victoria and the twins, but they were already halfway out the door. Maybe it was just as well, she thought, sinking into a chair at the dining table. She had no idea what to say, anyway. She needed to talk to Safet about how to approach this situation. Where on earth was he? He always gave her such a good perspective on things. She relied on his calm, clear logic.

As if on cue, he came into the kitchen. Finally.

'Morning.' She smiled, relief flooding through her. 'Where have you been?'

'I went for a little walk around the vineyard. There's a hiking trail we could do later, if you like?' He sniffed the air. 'Is that coffee I smell?'

'No, but it can be.' Ellie got up and clicked on the kettle. Then she grabbed the French press to make the coffee exactly as he liked it – brown sludge; the thicker the better.

He came over and poured himself a glass of water, and she admired his sinewy legs and arms. With his thick black hair, high cheekbones and a body as fit as it ever had been, he was an attractive man. She'd seen how other women looked at him, but he only seemed to have eyes for her. Sometimes, even now, she wondered why. She was nothing special: run-of-the-mill looks, average intelligence, not bad at most things but not great at any. Why had he got together with her in the first place? Was it because she was the first person who'd really listened to him? And why had he stayed? Because he'd believed there was nothing left in the place he still called home, where he'd always thought his real future would play out?

Guilt washed over her at the thought that that hadn't been exactly true. There had been someone from his past left, and he'd never known.

But she had.

Her mind flipped back to that day the doorbell had rung, so many years ago. She and Safet had moved into a small studio flat in Hackney, way before it had been cool. The flat was above a kebab shop on a dingy side street, drunks lurching in for a late-night feed forming the soundtrack to their sleep. They'd both been making peanuts, and it was all they could afford.

Safet had been at work one afternoon while she, having finished her shift at the café around the corner, tried to polish her CV yet again. Shockingly, no one wanted to hire a sociology graduate fresh out of school with no real-world experience, and she was getting frustrated working as a part-time waitress while Safet worked all hours at the refugee centre. And when someone from his home country came in needing help, he'd bring them back to the flat for food and a warm place to sleep. They'd talk for hours, laughing and joking in a language she had no hope of understanding.

That's what had led to their argument the evening before. Safet had been up all night with a man from the centre, and she'd been exhausted. She knew he missed Bosnia, but the flat was starting to feel more like an outpost of the centre and less like their home. In a rare outburst, fuelled by fatigue and frustration, she'd blurted that she might as well move back to her parents' place and leave him there. He'd looked at her with an expression that had immediately made shame zing through her. Because while she could go home, he never could.

'If that's what you want,' he'd said, and he'd gone into the bedroom and closed the door.

She'd tried all night to talk to him – to tell him she was sorry and it *wasn't* what she wanted at all – but he'd rolled over and gone to sleep. He'd headed to work the next morning without speaking to her, wearing his cold silence like a shield. With no idea if he even wanted to be with her anymore, she'd been left in agony. She loved him, and she'd thought that he loved her. But did he? And if he did love her, how could he shut her out so easily? His frozen face terrified her.

The doorbell had rung and, for a second, she'd thought it

might be him, that he'd forgotten his keys. She'd hit the buzzer before checking, then thrown open the door. But the woman at the door was a stranger, gazing at her with big dark eyes and a pale face.

'Can I help you?' Ellie had asked.

'I'm looking for Safet,' the woman said, her face tight. 'Safet Kovic? I heard he lived here?'

Ellie stepped back. 'Who are you?'

'I am a friend of his family,' the woman responded. 'Someone from his village. I am visiting relatives, and one of them mentioned his name. They said he lived here – that they'd stayed with him one night.'

'OK.' Ellie didn't want to give anything away until she spoke to Safet. He didn't talk much about the war, but the little he had told her made her understand that tensions from back home could sometimes spill over, across time and borders. This person must be OK if he'd stayed here, but she wasn't taking any chances.

'Is he here? I need to tell him something,' the woman said, her eyes wide. 'This is why I have come.'

Ellie shook her head. 'No, sorry. He's not here.'

The woman looked at her watch. 'I can't stay. I am going back to Bosnia this evening. But he needs to know...'

Ellie waited for the woman to speak, wondering what it was.

'His family.' The woman's stare went through her. 'They are all gone, but he had a cousin who went to fight, called Amir. He was ill for some time, and he was evacuated to a hospital in Germany. Everyone thought he was dead.'

She paused, and Ellie's heart started beating fast.

'But he's not. Amir is alive. He is in a special hospital back home and needs a lot of care, but he is alive.' She reached out and gripped Ellie's hand tightly. 'Please, please tell him that. This is the name of the hospital.' She handed

Ellie a piece of paper with a scribble on it that she could barely make out.

'I'll tell him.' Ellie's voice was hoarse.

'Thank you.' The woman nodded, then turned and left.

Amir is alive. Ellie stood in the middle of room, holding the paper in her hands as the woman's voice rang in her ears. Safet had always thought he had no family left. It was the reason he had come to England – because there was no one to stay for. He always said he never would have made the journey if there had been.

She had no doubt that when she gave him this paper, he would leave. He would go to see his cousin and, by the sounds of things, he'd need to stay. If Amir needed to be cared for, Safet would step up. Loyalty was everything to him, and this man was all he had left. She'd turned the piece of paper over and over in her hands, wondering for hours what to do.

She gave the memory a firm shove. That had been years ago. There was no point thinking of it when they had much bigger things to deal with... like Ahmed and Victoria.

'Why have you been texting Jules?' *Shit!* That hadn't been what she'd meant to say. The words slipped out, and she wanted to shake herself. She hadn't wanted to sound like that: suspicious, accusatory. The situation with the kids had thrown her.

'What?' Safet put down the glass of water, turning towards her.

'Nicola told me that you've been texting Jules a lot.' She tried to keep her voice even. 'I didn't think you two talked.'

Safet held her gaze, his dark eyes wide. 'Nicola? What else did she say?'

Ellie caught her breath as a stab of fear hit. 'Why? What else *is* there to say?' She'd expected him to laugh or joke, or *something*. Not to ask what else Nicola had told her. Why wasn't he rushing to reassure her?

She shifted, waiting for him to respond as panic gripped

her. Maybe she shouldn't have asked. She'd upset him – she never should have made it sound like an accusation. She knew how important trust was to him, and now she'd shown she didn't trust him. What had she been thinking?

She swallowed. 'Sorry. I'm sure it's nothing. You'll tell me if I need to know. I know you will. You go ahead on that hike if you want. Drink your coffee first, though!' Her voice was high and artificial, and she could tell by the way Safet was staring at her that she hadn't fooled him one bit. She poured the water from the kettle into the French press, then hurried from the room before he could say anything. She had to get out of here. Suddenly, all the emotions from so long ago – uncertainty, fear and the feeling she was never good enough – were threatening to flood in.

She'd thought she was over them, but they were closer than she'd realised. Maybe this place was bringing them back, she thought. No, she realised with a flash. It wasn't this place. It was these *people*. She'd tried so hard, but she'd never really fit in with them. And although she'd done so much and had a wonderful life now, she was still trying... with the same results. She'd been looking at those Uni years with rose-tinted glasses. While she'd loved that time with Safet, there'd never been many shared memories with the group to reminisce about in the first place. Even when they'd come here, they'd split off into their little units, like they were now.

She never should have organised this. She should have stayed in her London world, where people knew her and loved her. A few more days, she told herself. Get through the weekend, and then she could go home and be with the ones who really mattered: her family.

And now she had to find Ahmed and Victoria, and try her best to make it right.

NINE

JULES

Jules plopped onto a chair beside Harry, trying not to wince at the chocolate coating his lips from the pain au chocolat. All these years together and she'd never got used to the way her husband ate as if it was his very last meal and he had to ram the food down as quickly as possible. Those first few months after she'd had Ivy, when she'd been functioning on very little sleep, she'd dreamed of taking her baby away to a place where she'd never have to hear or see Harry chew again.

Luckily, once she'd managed to get some rest, she was able to cope. And in the grand scheme of things, it was such a minor annoyance. It would have been weird if he didn't have a quirk that irritated her. Really, Harry was still very much the same man she'd met that first day at Uni. She tilted her head, thinking of how she, Vannie and Ellie had been settling into their suite at the student halls, kitting out the shared kitchen with the dishes Jules had brought. Vannie had turned up with practically nothing, while Ellie's plates were cheap charity-shop ones, better suited to an eighty-year-old widow than the stylish Uni students they were now. Jules's mum had taken her on a no-holds-barred spree at Selfridges, where she'd chosen whatever she'd wanted without even looking at the price.

Harry had burst into the kitchen, full of confidence and swagger, kissing each of them on the cheek as he introduced himself before sitting and cracking open a beer as they unpacked. Typical male, Vannie had said as she rolled her eyes, grabbing a beer from the fridge herself and plonking onto the chair next to his, refusing to carry on while he was sitting idle. Jules could feel his eyes on her, watching appreciatively as she swung from the box to the cupboard, flicking her long blonde hair over her shoulder. It was as if they were playing roles, and she knew how to play that game. It was a game she'd grown up watching her mother play with her father, and they'd had such a wonderful marriage – until, for some unfathomable reason, her mother had left.

Pain curled through her as Jules remembered coming home from Uni for Christmas, only to find her mother packing up her things as her father begged and pleaded for her to stay. Jules had joined her father's pleas, asking with increasing desperation why her mum was doing this. But her mother had shaken her head and pressed her lips together, then hugged Jules close and said they'd talk later.

Christmas came and went in a blur of drunken parties, and Jules still hadn't heard from her mother, despite calling over and over. One day after New Year's, she'd rung her mum's phone to leave a message, only to find it dead. She couldn't say why, but alarm bells went off, a feeling a dread lodged inside. She'd called Vannie, who was interning at a place close to her mum's Soho hotel, and left an urgent message for her to check on her mother. Then she jumped in a cab, telling herself she was overreacting yet still with that pounding dread inside. She'd raced up to the room, and when she'd seen the door ajar, her heart had dropped. Something was wrong: very wrong. Had there been an intruder, maybe? Had they hurt her mother? There had to be some reason the door had been left open...

Legs trembling, she'd crept into the room, her heart beating fast as she scanned the small space. The bed was neatly made, her mum's suitcase was still in the corner, and her clothes still hung in the wardrobe. The only sound was the drip of water from the bathroom.

And somehow... somehow, she'd known.

Jules knew she would never get that horrific image out of her head. It lingered, waiting there behind her eyelids, every time she closed her eyes. For months – years – she'd fought off sleep, succumbing only when she'd had so much booze she was practically comatose. The pain of losing her mother was the worst thing she'd ever experienced. She'd never even had the chance to say goodbye.

It was part of the reason why Frederick leaving so suddenly had hurt so much. He hadn't said goodbye either. It made her feel hollow, expendable, as if she was someone people could turn their backs on. But Vannie hadn't. Harry hadn't either. They'd made a life together, and she'd be forever grateful.

'Jules.' Harry turned towards her, wiping his mouth, and she tried not to notice how the trail of chocolate had transferred to his hand. 'Listen.'

She raised her eyebrows at his serious tone. The last time he'd looked like this had been when she'd found out about the twins. But he couldn't have done anything like that again. She'd seen how sorry he'd been; how much he'd regretted it. Could he have found out her plans with Safet, maybe? No, surely not. God, she needed to talk to him. She'd texted again, but he'd said he was out for a walk and they could chat later.

'Is everything OK?' Her head was throbbing. She really needed a drink.

'Oh yes, it's fine.' He squeezed her hand. 'But I want to discuss something with you.'

Discuss something? Well, this was a turn-up for the books. Usually, Harry made the decisions and told her later. And while it might not be very progressive of her, she liked it that way; liked feeling cared for. Was it something to do with his job, maybe? But she couldn't remember him ever talking to her about that – well, besides that last year in Uni when he'd asked if her father could find him a job in his company. Her dad had loved Harry, so he'd said yes in a heartbeat. He'd be retiring in a few years, he'd laughed, and he had to start training up his successor. He'd been joking, of course, but Jules had seen the spark of ambition in Harry's eyes, and she'd loved it. Harry had fit in perfectly, going from strength to strength – and the fact that he was the husband of the founder's daughter helped, of course.

'What is it?' she asked.

'I've been thinking, well... Now that Ivy has moved out, it might be time to downsize. Buy a cosy little flat for the two of us next to the Heath or something. We don't need to rattle around in such a big place, do we? I thought we could list it when we get home.'

Jules's mouth dropped open. How long had he been thinking about this? He loved their house. Despite the fact that her father was covering the cost, he was the one who'd insisted on buying such a big place, saying they'd need the space for all the children she was going to give them. That might not have happened, but the thought of selling their house was unimaginable.

'What do you think?' he asked. He reached down, and Jules's eyes bulged when she saw the thick stack of paperwork he'd hidden behind the newspaper. 'I had the house valued last week, and I'm ready to instruct the estate agent. I need you to sign a few things, since it's your name on the deed. If you sign now, I can call the agent and he can even get it on the market today. Exciting, eh?'

Jules stared, trying to take in his words. *Wow.* He'd had it valued already? And he wanted her to sign this second? Not much of a discussion, then, was it? She glanced at the papers. Harry hadn't been thrilled when her father had insisted on a prenuptial and keeping the house in her name, but he knew she'd never leave him. After what happened with her mother, he understood how desperately she'd wanted a family.

'Right,' she said slowly. Maybe it was a good idea. The house did seem too big lately. 'It's definitely something worth thinking about,' she said. 'But we need to talk about it more. I—'

'Have you seen Ahmed?' Ellie appeared from behind them, her face twisted with worry. 'I've looked everywhere, but there's no sign of him. He got upset and ran off.'

Harry waved a hand. 'Calm down. I'm sure he'll come out again when he's ready.'

But Ellie looked anything but calm. 'He's not like other kids,' she said. 'He can't cope with emotions – he simply shuts down. Usually, he goes into the bathroom, since it's the one sure place with a lock. Or in closets, under tables... anywhere it's dark. But I checked, and he's not in any of those places. I need to find him.' She looked up at the sky. 'Before it starts to rain.'

Jules glanced up, noticing with surprise that the early-morning sun had vanished and dark clouds were gathering. A wind was whipping the humid air around them, and the whole atmosphere felt heavy and laden as if the sky was about to crack open.

'Please can you help?' Ellie looked frantic, her eyes huge. 'I'd really appreciate it.'

'OK.' Jules got to her feet. 'We can talk about this later, all right?' she said, looking down at Harry.

It was clear he wasn't happy about the interruption, but he nodded. 'I'll stay here in case he comes this way.' Harry leaned back in his chair, picking up the newspaper again.

Jules followed Ellie towards the back of the property, where they could see Frederick peering into one of the outbuildings dotted around the perimeter. Jules sighed, watching him. She'd wait until Ahmed was found, and then she'd ask him to go.

'Vannie and Nicola are checking through the house again,' Ellie said, breathless, 'but I think he's out here somewhere. I told the girls to stay in the annex while we look. The last thing we want is to lose one of them trying to find Ahmed.'

Jules nodded, wondering what had got him so upset. Unlike Ivy, whose emotions she knew in an instant, Ahmed was so hard to read. He hardly looked at her, and when she tried to talk to him, he shied away. Had the twins said something to him? God, she hoped not. If Ivy had been here, she would have taken Ahmed under her wing, and Nat and Mia would have responded in kind.

'I know you think I'm being ridiculous,' Ellie said, her face creased with worry as they walked around the perimeter of the villa's grounds. 'I know he's eleven, and he's not a baby. But he's been through so much.'

Jules put a hand on Ellie's arm. 'Hey, you don't need to explain anything. Even if it was Ivy – who, God knows, is well able to take care of herself – I'd want to make sure she was OK.'

Ellie nodded, and despite the distance between them, Jules felt a zing of connection. She and Ellie had always got on. It was impossible *not* to get on with her, since she always seemed afraid of making waves. But they'd never connected, even after living together for so long in university. It was hard to see behind the eagerness to please to how Ellie actually felt, and sometimes, Jules secretly wondered how Safet had taken that all these years. But now, Ellie's love shone through so clearly that Jules could see who she was beyond the pliable person she presented.

'He's not in any of those buildings.' Frederick came towards them, and Jules turned. His face was flushed with the heat and his hair was damp with sweat at his temples. 'Could he have gone into the forest, do you think? There's a trail that cuts through there.' He gestured towards the trees lining the grounds. In the greying light with the wind howling around them, the trees seemed more ominous than the inviting wood they'd driven through to get here.

'I don't think so,' Ellie said.

'Safet's walking out there at the moment, so he might spot him if he is,' Jules said.

Ellie darted a look at Jules at the mention of her husband's name, then glanced away with an expression Jules couldn't interpret. Did she know something? Had Safet talked to her? No, he wouldn't. Not without speaking to Jules first.

Vannie and Nicola approached them, shaking their heads. 'We couldn't find him inside the house. That place is huge, though, with so many nooks and crannies. It'd take hours to search thoroughly.'

'Well, maybe he's hiding over there.' Frederick pointed towards a pile of old stone blocks. 'Let's go see, and then we can take another look in the villa.' He looked up at the sky, growing darker by the second. 'Better inside than out here.'

They hurried down a slope towards the stones, stopping in front of them and staring as steps cut into the ground and a large wooden door came into sight.

'What is this?' Ellie asked.

'Looks like it's an old cellar or something,' Frederick said. 'Might have been for storing wine. Some of these old vineyards had huge underground spaces. Could be a whole labyrinth under there.'

Jules shivered at the thought of the dark, narrow tunnels twisting underground.

Ellie rushed down the stairs and tried to open the door, but it held firm. 'Can you help me? I really want to check inside. This is the kind of place he'd love.'

Frederick gripped the rusty handle and pulled hard, but

nothing happened. He jerked the door back and forth, then jiggled the handle, and it flew open.

'Ahmed? Ahmed! Are you in there?'

They all listened intently, straining to hear, but there was nothing.

'Ahmed?' Ellie called into the darkness.

Jules thought she heard a rustle in the corner. She pointed silently towards the noise, praying it was Ahmed and not a rat or something equally unpleasant. She watched as Ellie slowly approached a dark shape huddled in the corner. Ahmed streaked into Ellie's arms, and she rocked him back and forth. The love between them was palpable and brought tears to Jules's eyes. God, she missed Ivy.

'Come on. Let's get you inside before it starts raining,' Ellie said. Outside, fat drops were beginning to fall from the sky. 'Raining harder, anyway. I hope Safet's back.'

'Me too,' Jules said, glancing up at the sky. 'But if not, I'm sure he's on his way home. And later today, Ellie... maybe we can have a chat? I... well, Safet and I have something to tell you.' She bit her lip, thinking she did need to talk to Safet first, like he'd said. But she was desperate now to move forward; to think about her future.

Ellie stiffened, and Jules regretted mentioning it this soon after finding Ahmed. She was already so tense.

'Sure,' she said, her voice higher than normal. 'Come on, Ahmed.' She turned towards him and beckoned him forward before starting up the stairs. Ahmed trailed behind as if reluctant to leave.

'Wow.' Frederick shone the torch from his mobile around the space. 'This is amazing.'

Despite not wanting to stay in the small dark place with a man from her past she was trying to escape, Jules couldn't help gazing around the cavern. The stone floor was littered with old wooden barrels and crates, and the air was warm and musty, a different climate than the one outside. A low stone ceiling arched over them, and Jules stepped further inside, trying to put more distance between her and Frederick. How far back did it go?

She was about to take another step forward when the door slammed behind her and the darkness fell like a curtain. She froze. Had Frederick locked her in here? Surely he wouldn't do something like that, she told herself, trying to calm her pounding heart as the black swirled around her.

'Hello?' she called out, praying someone could hear her.

'I'm here.'

Frederick's voice filled the space, and she froze once more. The only thing worse than being in here on her own was being here with him. Had he shut the door? God, how far would he go to talk to her? Anger swarmed through her.

'Frederick, this isn't funny,' she said, her voice shaking. 'Open the door and get us out.'

'I didn't close it,' he said, his voice calm. 'It must have been the wind. Stay still while I turn on the torch on my mobile phone.'

She heard him fumble around, and then a faint glow appeared.

He aimed the light in the direction of the door. 'Hang on a second while I make my way over to it. There's so much stuff crammed inside here.' He swore as he knocked over a pile of crates that crashed to the floor, blocking their path.

She navigated through the dim space, sweating and covered with dust as they heaved the heavy wooden boxes out of their way. After what felt like forever, Frederick reached the door. He grabbed the rusted handle and pushed, but nothing happened. He threw his weight against the door, but still it remained fast. What the hell? Why wasn't it opening?

'Let me try,' she said. There was no way she was going to be trapped in here with this man.

Frederick shrugged and stepped back, shining the light so she could find her way over. She gripped the handle and tried with all her might, but it wouldn't budge. In the dim light, the shadows playing on Frederick's face made him look like a stranger, and she shivered.

'I'll call Ellie,' Frederick said, peering in the darkness at the phone. 'She can come let us out from the other side. Hopefully, it's not jammed.'

Jules nodded, wrapping her arms around herself.

'Oh, shit.' He stared at the mobile. 'I don't have a signal in here. What about you?'

Jules took out her phone, ducking her head to try to see the screen. 'No, I don't have one either.'

'Right. Must be because we're underground and the stone walls are so thick.' They stared at each other, then Frederick pulled a crate over and gestured for her to sit. 'Might as well make ourselves comfortable. At least we're out of the storm. Ellie knows where we are. When she realises we haven't come back, she'll come get us. Hopefully, it won't take long. And in the meantime... maybe we can talk?'

Jules swallowed, edging away. No. No way.

The sooner they got out of here, the better.

TEN
ELLIE

'Ahmed?' Ellie paused in the pouring rain as she crossed the field, biting her lip as she spotted Ahmed trailing behind her. He was usually right beside her, but clearly he'd overheard what Victoria said and it had affected him. She waited as he came towards her, his whole body shaking and his face tight with tension. It reminded her of the first day they'd seen him at the refugee centre, how he'd been standing there, rooted to the ground with a face like a statue. The only thing that had given him away was the trembling of his body.

She'd gone straight to him, and even though she knew she shouldn't, she'd pulled him in for a huge hug. He'd tensed even more and she'd wondered if she'd made a mistake, but then he'd relaxed and clung onto her, his chest heaving with sobs. She'd known then that she couldn't ever let him go.

She pulled him inside the villa and handed him a towel from the pile by the door to the pool. 'I know you're upset because of what the girls said,' she began gently, watching as tears filled his eyes. 'Don't worry. We'll figure it out.'

He turned to her. 'I wasn't filming them. I promise.'

'Maybe not. But it might have looked that way to them.'

Ellie sighed. 'I've been thinking... maybe it's best if you give the phone to me for safekeeping.'

Fear and panic crossed Ahmed's face, and he jerked away. 'No. No, please.'

Ellie sighed again. 'All right. But at least keep the phone away from the girls, OK?'

Ahmed nodded, his face full of relief.

'And, Ahmed, Victoria does love you. People sometimes say things when they're upset; things they don't mean. She does want you here. I can promise you that.' She smiled gently at him, but his face was still tight with tension.

'You want me too, right?' he asked. Her heart almost broke. 'You and Safet? Our family... we will be OK?'

Ellie blinked. 'Of course,' she said, even though her tone sounded uncertain to her ears. She tilted her head, wondering why he was worried. Fear leapt into her as a thought hit. Had he seen something? Something to do with Jules and Safet? She took the towel from him, her mind working. Nicola had mentioned seeing messages on Jules's phone last night. Could Ahmed have spotted some on Safet's?

A huge clap of thunder made them both jump, and Ellie turned towards him. 'You stay with Vannie and Nicola while I talk to your sister. Everything will be fine.' She tried to inject as much confidence and reassurance as she could into her voice, but Ahmed continued to gaze at her with wide, fearful eyes. She could tell she hadn't convinced him and that he didn't want to leave her, but the sky was growing dark and the wind was gathering strength, and she wanted him safely inside the villa.

Vannie was crouched in the corner of the lounge practically glued to her phone, while Nicola was staring at her own mobile with a face like thunder. What was the point of coming all this way if you only saw the same thing in front of you: a screen? But Vannie had always been like that, intense and focused. When she wanted something, she got it... like being best friends with

Jules. Ellie remembered how she and Jules had been chatting that first day at Uni, getting to know one another. Jules had seemed so friendly, asking question after question to break through her shyness as her parents put away the vast amount of things she'd brought. Then Vannie had come in on her own and plonked down her small case, almost as if she owned the place. She'd said a cursory hello to Ellie before turning to Jules and her parents with a megawatt grin and a confident handshake. Ellie had slunk off to her room, leaving the four of them laughing like old friends in the kitchen. The dynamic had continued all through their years, but it hadn't bothered her after she'd got together with Safet.

She shouldn't have expected anything different this time around. Anyway, it didn't matter, she reminded herself. All she needed was to focus on her family.

'Can Ahmed stay with you for a second while I talk to Victoria?' she asked.

Vannie nodded and patted the seat beside her, and Ahmed eased down gingerly as if Vannie was a bomb about to go off.

Out by the pool under the canopy, despite the wind flapping the canvas and the rain falling from the sky, Harry was staring intently at his phone, a mirror image of Vannie. As she crossed to the annex, Ellie gazed at the trees in the distance, wondering where the hell Safet was. Jules's words that they needed to talk echoed in her mind, and she shivered. Talk about what, exactly? She'd been chastising herself over and over for bringing up the texts with Safet. But... she swallowed as she pictured the look on his face. He hadn't denied it. He hadn't tried to explain it. *Was* there something going on?

She shook away the question and went inside the annex to check on the girls. The twins were there, but Victoria wasn't with them.

'Where's Victoria?' she asked.

They didn't even look up from their phones as they

shrugged. Sighing, she walked slowly through the kitchen which now resembled a disaster zone where every plate had been used, then stuck her head inside Victoria's bedroom.

'Vic?' she called. 'Are you in here?'

But the bedroom was empty, and she couldn't stop herself from walking inside and sinking onto the bed. Clothes were strewn over it, and Ellie raised an eyebrow as she spotted a hot-pink bra with mesh cups. What on earth? She certainly hadn't bought that for her daughter. Could Victoria have borrowed it from the twins? The thought of her wearing something so sexy made discomfort prick her insides.

Her daughter's old teddy was half-hidden under some discarded clothes, and Ellie picked it up. It was missing an eye and the fur was nubbly and worn, but Victoria still brought it everywhere. It was a reminder that, as much as she wanted to be an adult, part of her was still a child.

Ellie stared at the bear, wondering if she'd expected too much from her daughter. When they'd first talked to Victoria about Ahmed joining their family, she'd been all for it. She'd hated being an only child, and even when she'd been young, she'd constantly asked Ellie to have another baby. The plea had brought tears to her eyes, because as much as she and Safet had longed for it, it hadn't happened. Ahmed was a chance for Victoria to be the older sister she'd always wanted to be.

But the reality had been different. Ahmed had been shy and fearful, clinging to Ellie and Safet. He didn't want to play Xbox or Roblox or any of the things Victoria had done growing up. He was an alien, someone Victoria couldn't relate to, and she'd begun to withdraw from him – and them – spending all her time in her room.

Ellie had checked in with Victoria's form teacher to make sure the changes at home weren't affecting her grades, and she'd got a positive report. She'd tried to talk to Victoria about how she was feeling, but her only response was eye-rolls and grunts.

She'd known it had been tricky with Ahmed, and that she and Safet had paid him a lot of attention, but... She shifted on the soft bed, remembering Victoria's words; the anger and hurt that had tainted her normally soft voice. Victoria had been hurting a lot more than Ellie had realised.

They'd have a chat when Ellie found her. An open and honest discussion, like they used to when Victoria was younger. Her family was strong – she'd always prided herself on their tight little unit. Whatever was happening with Ahmed and Victoria; whatever was going on with Safet... she'd sort it out. It wasn't going to fall apart now, here of all places.

Ellie ducked outside once more, thinking Victoria couldn't be far – she hated her hair getting wet, and it was raining harder than ever. She circled the perimeter of the property again, the same way she had when she was looking for Ahmed. She was about to pass by the cellar where Ahmed had been stuck when she heard banging and shouting. She paused, straining to listen. What on earth? Could Victoria be trapped in there? But how? Had she gone in after Ahmed had come out, maybe?

She yanked the door, but it didn't budge, and her heart sank. Oh God, not again. And this time, she didn't have Frederick's strength to help. But... she put her head closer to the door as she heard voices inside. That didn't sound like Victoria. It was a man's voice.

'Who's in there?' she called, as loudly as she could.

'It's Jules and Frederick.' Jules's voice was faint through the heavy door.

'Is Victoria with you?' she asked.

'No. Can you get us out?'

'I'm trying!' She yanked the door once more, almost jerking her arm from its socket. But it still didn't give way.

She wiped the rain from her face and peered at the rusty handle. Somehow, the old locking mechanism seemed to have been engaged. No wonder it wouldn't open, she thought, examining the worn parts. They'd jiggled it so much trying to free Ahmed that she supposed anything could have happened.

'It looks like it's locked!' she yelled as loudly as she could. 'I think there's a key in the house. I'll be back in a second, OK?' She dashed back towards the villa, nearly jumping out of her skin as another massive boom of thunder overhead made everything shake. Where on earth was Safet? And where was her daughter?

She slammed the door behind her and stood dripping in the foyer, trying to slough off as much water as she could.

'What's going on?' Vannie's voice came from the lounge.

Ellie hurried in. At least Ahmed was safe, curled up in the corner of the sofa with his phone.

'Bit of a situation,' she said, trying to make it seem like all this would be part of some great story later. 'Somehow Frederick and Jules are stuck in the cellar.'

'*What?* Together?' Vannie's eyebrows rose.

Nicola let out a snort. 'Wow,' she said. 'Things just got interesting. A whole cellar full of wine for Jules to get drunk on. You better get her out of there fast.'

'They went in to have a look after we found Ahmed,' Ellie said, ignoring Nicola's words. 'Somehow the door closed and the old lock engaged. I need to find a key to get them out again.' She ran a hand through her hair. 'When we arrived, the manager told me there's a ring of keys for all the outbuildings, but he said we wouldn't need them. I think they're in the foyer, above the coat rack.' She made a face. 'Or something like that. I wasn't really listening, to be honest. I'll check if they're there now.'

Vannie nodded, and Ellie turned to go.

'Ouf!' She ran straight into her daughter, and relief swamped her. 'Oh, thank goodness.' She gathered Victoria in her arms, trying not to notice how hers stayed by her sides instead of gripping her back. 'I've been looking everywhere for you!' she said, pushing a lock of damp hair from her daughter's forehead. She was absolutely dripping. Where had she been?

'Before or after you found Ahmed?' Victoria asked, her eyes wide and full of anger.

Oh God. 'Well, he was in such a state, and he's younger than you. I know you didn't mean it, but your words hurt him.' Ellie stared at her daughter, desperately trying to think of the right words to say. When had this become so difficult?

'Right.' The tears in Victoria's eyes were at odds with her defiant expression. 'What a surprise: he comes first. Well, don't worry. I've got people who do pay attention to me.'

She spun away, and Ellie stood for a minute. What did she mean? The twins? Her friends at school? There was a time when Ellie knew everything about her daughter's little gang. Now, she hardly knew anyone.

They would need to have that heart-to-heart, but first she had to get Jules and Frederick out of the cellar. At least they were dry and out of the storm, which was more than she could say for her husband. Maybe he'd taken refuge in the village until it passed, she thought. He could have at least called her, though. A thought sprang into her head, and she flinched. Had he called *Jules*? Was that how Jules had known he was out walking? And what on earth did they want to talk to her about? She couldn't believe he'd do anything to hurt her, but...

Right, one problem at a time. She took a deep breath as she walked into the foyer where the manager had said the keys were. There was a hook above the coat rack, but no keys were on it. Ellie sighed, wishing she'd paid more attention. She'd call now to double-check. She found the plastic pouch with all the information in it and rang the number for the property manager, praying he would pick up.

'*Oui, allô?*'

Oh, thank God. 'Yes, it's Ellie Kovic. I'm at the villa and there are two people trapped in an old wine cellar in the field behind the villa. It looks like the lock is engaged. You mentioned a key ring, but I can't find it.'

She furrowed her brows as the manager told her in his thick French accent where the key ring was hanging, repeating it back to him to ensure she'd got it right. The hook above the coat rack, but... she looked again. They definitely weren't there.

'There's nothing,' she said. 'A hook, yes, but no keys.'

He let out a puff of air. 'They are there. You must look again.'

She glanced back up at the hook, hoping they would magically appear. 'No, nothing.'

'*Merde.* The cleaners must not have put them back,' he said. 'They store their things in one of the buildings. Sometimes, they take the keys with them. I did not think to check.'

'Well, what am I supposed to do?' Ellie's voice was rising. This wasn't an amusing anecdote any longer.

'The cleaners are away until next week, but I will call a locksmith. It may take some time, though. At least your friends have wine.' He let out a low laugh.

Ellie grimaced. She wasn't sure they would find that funny.

'In the meantime, make sure the rest of you stay inside,' he was continuing. 'This storm, it will be bad.'

Ellie nodded and hung up, thinking at least she could try to talk to her daughter now.

If only she could talk to her husband too.

ELEVEN

JULES

Jules shivered in the dark as she sat on an old crate. It was so black in the cellar that, without the glow from the mobile, she couldn't tell if her eyes were open or closed. The dark made Frederick's breathing seem even louder; the warmth of his body more intense. He was across the cellar on another crate, but he still felt too close. She shook her head, thinking how ironic it was that the one person she'd wanted to avoid was the person she was trapped in here with. She should have asked him to leave when she'd had the chance. Now, there was nowhere to run and nowhere to hide.

There was a load of old wine, though. But as much as she wanted to drink it, she needed a clear head to deal with the man beside her. She couldn't let any old emotions cloud her mind; couldn't slip back into her memories like last night. Because they *were* old emotions, she reminded herself. She wasn't that young girl, and she didn't know the man beside her. She'd never really known him in the first place if he could talk about a future together, then take off the very next day. No matter what he wanted to tell her now, she didn't need to hear it. He probably only wanted to say it to feel better about how he'd behaved.

A boom of thunder shook the thick stone walls of the cellar, and Jules looked upwards automatically, even though she knew she couldn't see the sky.

'Jules, I want to respect your wishes not to talk. I don't want to hurt you... hurt you more.'

Frederick's voice was full of pain, and Jules's eyebrows rose in surprise. Why did he sound that way? He was the one who had left.

'But I can't move on, knowing what happened because of that night. How it changed my life – *your* life. How it changed everything.'

Jules stiffened. Yes, his leaving had changed the course of her life, but how could it have changed his? He'd been planning to travel, anyway. What was he talking about?

'There's nothing I can say to tell you how sorry I am for what happened.' Frederick's voice was low and intense. 'Nothing at all. I'm grateful that you had Vannie there with you. It seems like she's been a true friend to you – the friend I wish I could have been.' His tone went raspy. 'I know she was only trying to protect you when she asked me to leave that morning.'

What? Jules jerked. *Vannie* told him to leave? Why the hell would she have done that? No. Not in a million years. Vannie would have told her. He must be making this up to try to make himself look better.

Her mind flashed back to that morning when she'd awoken to find Frederick gone. She'd padded downstairs, the smell of coffee wrapping around her. Vannie had handed her a steaming mug.

'Good morning!' She'd smiled brightly at Jules, who went over and gave her a hug. 'Oh, what's that for?'

Jules shrugged. 'Just feeling happy today.' A sunbeam went through her, and for the first time since she'd arrived at the villa, it felt airy and bright, not oppressive. Someone loved her.

Someone wanted to have her in their life. She didn't need to feel alone anymore. 'Where's Frederick?'

'Frederick?' Vannie handed her the milk. 'Oh, he had to go. Early flight or something.'

'What?' Jules's heart dropped so fast it felt as if her legs were going to give out. It couldn't be true. She couldn't have heard Vannie properly. 'He's gone?'

Vannie nodded, and Jules continued to stare. 'Did he... did he say anything?' Maybe he'd left a note or a message for Vannie to pass on. He must have done. They couldn't have finally got together, only for him to take off. She knew he loved her. She felt it in every single cell. If she didn't trust Frederick, then she couldn't trust anyone. Well, other than Vannie, of course.

Vannie met her eyes. 'He said to tell you he was sorry,' she said softly, and Jules slumped onto a chair. Tears came to her eyes and she swiped them away with the back of her hand. This couldn't be happening. It was like a bad dream. 'That he was drunk and he shouldn't have kissed you.'

Jules's insides had churned with pain, and Vannie sat down beside her and put a hand on her back. 'But he wanted you to know that he didn't do anything more. He realised how out of it you both were, and he knew it wasn't right. Anyway, he didn't want to cause problems with you and Harry.'

Harry. Jules remembered the fight they'd had last night, and anger jolted through her.

'Harry's crashed out on the sofa,' Vannie continued. 'You don't have to worry – he didn't see Frederick leave. He really loves you, Jules. He said he's sorry about last night. He does want to be with you.'

Jules had sat there as Vannie's voice washed over her, trying to absorb everything. Why had Frederick taken off without even saying goodbye? How could he make her think he wanted her – *loved* her – and then go? He'd been the one person to gaze beyond the golden exterior to the person underneath. He'd seen

her at her absolute lowest, and he'd helped raise her up. She'd
trusted him with her heart, and he'd left. She bent over as her
head throbbed and nausea rose inside, but it wasn't down to the
amount of alcohol she'd drunk. It was the pain of having
someone she loved ripped from her.

Again.

She took in a few deep breaths, trying to grab onto something solid. Frederick was gone. Harry was here. Yes, they'd had
a big fight and he'd said awful things. But she hadn't been the
best girlfriend lately either, with everything that had happened
with her mum and how much time she'd spent with Frederick.
It was a wonder Harry hadn't broken up with *her*, actually.
Guilt flooded in, mixed with relief that nothing had happened
with Frederick. Thank God she'd passed out.

She'd spent the rest of the day in a daze, smiling lamely at
Harry and downing drink after drink. When he'd asked if she
wanted to move in with him, she'd nodded numbly. She'd tried
her best to lean into him once more, pushing the hurt and pain
way down deep inside.

A knock at the cellar door jerked her back to the present.
'I've spoken to the manager of the house, and he thinks the
cleaners took the keys by accident.' They could barely hear
Ellie's soft voice through the thick stone walls, and Frederick
groaned. 'So you might be stuck inside there a little longer, OK?
He's trying to find a locksmith to come. Hopefully, you'll be out
in a few hours.'

A few *hours*? Oh God. She had to get out of here now. She
didn't want to hear any more of Frederick's twisted version of
the past.

'Are the kids OK? Is everyone else safe inside? Safe?' She
hoped he wasn't still out on his walk in what sounded like brutal
weather.

'The kids are fine.' Ellie's voice had a strange tone to it now
– or was Jules imagining it? 'Don't worry. Right, I'm going to

head back to the house. It's absolutely torrential out here. I'll keep you posted.'

Silence descended again, and Frederick's words echoed in her head, stirring up more and more anger with every second. 'You don't need to say that Vannie asked you to go. You don't need to blame someone else.' Jules's voice burst out of her. 'Say the truth. You left because you wanted to.'

'Because I wanted to?' Frederick's laugh was incredulous. 'You couldn't be more off the mark. I left that night because of what I did.' His voice went low and dark, and she could hear the pain and anger. 'Did to *you*. That was the only reason.'

TWELVE
VANNIE

Vannie stared at the mobile screen, not seeing anything through the fear curdling her insides. Where oh where was that locksmith? She had to get Jules out of there – sooner rather than later. The mobile started ringing, and she jerked in surprise as the name came up. It was Ivy. Had she tried to reach Jules and been unable to get through? Jules answered her daughter's calls without fail; Vannie always thought how lucky Ivy was to have such a dedicated mother. She hadn't spoken to hers for years, an arrangement that seemed to work for them both. Jules's mum had been a stand-in for her, taking Vannie under her wing and checking in on her as if she were her daughter.

Once, when Vannie had been very ill with glandular fever, she'd even gone to stay at Jules's parents' place for a couple of weeks to avoid infecting the rest of the house. Despite how ill she'd been, it had been one of the best times of her life. She could still feel Anita's cool hand on her forehead; how they'd watched TV together in the dim light of the room. For a while, Vannie could almost believe that this was her mother and her home. When she'd died... Vannie drew in a breath, holding back the grief and guilt still waiting to overwhelm her. How she wished she could turn back time to tell her younger self that being close to someone didn't fill the gaps that existed in her life. That they could only cause new ones. New ones that created even more pain.

'Hey, Vannie.' Ivy's voice came through the line and, despite everything, Vannie smiled. It was so nice to hear from her. 'I've been trying to reach Mum, but her mobile doesn't seem like it's connecting. It keeps going straight to voicemail.'

'Oh, it's probably the service here. It's quite spotty.' There was no need to upset Ivy by telling her the truth. 'Is everything OK?'

'Yes, it's fine.' The line went silent for a second. 'It's... well, there's something I want to talk to her about. And you too.'

'Oh.' Vannie drew back. What could it be? Ivy's voice was serious, so different to her normal light tone. Fear wormed in. Could she be ill? Oh God. Please may she not be ill. 'Are you sure you're OK?'

Ivy laughed, and Vannie felt relief wash over her.

'Calm down, calm down. God, you're worse than Mum! I'm fine, I promise.'

'Good.' Vannie let out a breath. Ivy was everything. She couldn't bear it if anything happened to her.

'I'll see you soon, anyway. We can chat about it then.'

'We'll be back in a couple of days,' Vannie said. 'Shall we arrange a time to meet?'

'No, no.' Ivy laughed. 'I'm here now.'

Vannie jerked. 'You're *what*?'

'I'm at the airport in Bordeaux. I just landed. Sorry to spring this on you, but I thought it might be a good place to talk. Neutral ground, and you guys are all in the same place at once, you know? Anyway, I can't wait any longer.'

Vannie was still struggling to take in what Ivy had said. She was here? Now? And *why* couldn't she wait any longer? It must be something big if she had to fly to another country to talk... talk to Vannie... talk to her mum. And Ivy was fine, so it wasn't her health. It couldn't be relationship issues either. She wasn't dating anyone seriously, only that boy she'd called a fuck buddy. She'd gone on and on about how great the sex was, and Vannie had laughingly told her to stop talking about it, but to make sure she was staying safe.

Vannie froze. Could Ivy be pregnant? Could that be it? Maybe that's why she'd been keeping her distance from Jules and Vannie these past few months: because she'd been afraid to tell them.

'But I can't find anyone who will drive me out to the villa,' Ivy was saying. 'No taxis want to go any further than Bordeaux, in case the weather gets worse.'

'I'll pick you up,' Vannie said quickly. 'Give me an hour. I'll be there as fast as I can.' Going now, with Jules and Frederick trapped in the cellar, wasn't ideal, but she couldn't leave Ivy stranded at the airport. By the sounds of things, it might take a while until the manager found someone who could open the door. Hopefully, she could get back here for when Jules got out, in time to make sure she was OK after being locked away with Frederick. She was bound to be rattled, and Vannie would be there for her. As always.

'Great,' Ivy said. 'That will give me a chance to talk to you before I speak to Mum. A dry run for what I'm going to say. I'll see you soon.'

Vannie swallowed as she hung up the phone. Now, it wasn't just Jules and Frederick to worry about. Or bloody Harry, still having the nerve to ask her for favours. Now, it was Ivy, too, in the middle of the storm. How much worse could things get?

'I'm going to the village to see if I can find a locksmith,' she said to Ellie, the lie coming smoothly from her mouth. The last thing anyone needed right now was to worry about another person in the midst of this weather. 'We shouldn't rely on the manager's word.' She glanced around the room. Where had

Nicola gone? 'Can you tell Nicola I'll be back soon?' Her girl-friend wouldn't be pleased. She was still sulking over how much time Vannie had spent with Jules last night, but Vannie had to do this for her god-daughter... and for Jules. Together, they were her life.

Ellie was shaking her head. 'The manager said we shouldn't go anywhere. I'm worried about Safet.' She glanced out the window. 'He's not answering his mobile. I don't know where he's got to, and the storm's getting worse.'

Vannie grabbed the car keys, shoving down irritation. Safet was a grown man. He could take care of himself. Couldn't Ellie exist for five minutes without him? She made a face, remembering how Ellie had always been stuck to his side at Uni as if he'd disappear if she let him out of her sight. He *would* disappear one day if she kept that up.

'I'll be fine,' she said. 'He will be too. Don't worry, every-thing will be OK.'

She ran through the rain to the car, then drove as quickly as she could down the narrow lane towards the village. The wind whipped the trees on either side of the road and the rain sluiced down the windscreen, reducing visibility to almost zero. Even Vannie had to admit that, in any other circumstances, there was no way she'd risk driving.

But this wasn't just any circumstance. This was her god-daughter, and she'd do whatever she could to make sure she stayed safe – safe from anything that might hurt her, the same way she had for Jules that night so long ago... and beyond. Sometimes, she still couldn't believe she *had* managed to keep quiet about what had really happened at the villa. It had affected everything, the consequences spilling out until this day. Only she knew, and she had to keep it that way.

She bit her lip, wondering if she was right and Ivy was pregnant. Like Jules had been, still so young with so much ahead of her. When Jules had told her she was pregnant,

Vannie had been shocked. How the hell could she be so stupid? A baby would ruin everything. She'd hidden her panic, though, raking through her mind to come up with the right response. She'd told Jules she'd be beside her every step of the way. She'd book the appointment, take her there, and hold her hand afterwards. No one besides Vannie needed to know – particularly not Harry, who'd run a mile. He always joked he wore two condoms, just in case. Vannie would roll her eyes, remembering Jules telling her about his very lax approach to contraception.

But... Vannie had swallowed, a thought entering her mind. Maybe this was what would get rid of Harry. If he found out Jules was having his baby, he'd be off like a rocket. Jules would decide not to have it, and that would be that. He'd be out of the picture, for once and for all. And his departure from Jules's life would set Vannie free too. Free from what he knew. Free from his threats to ruin everything.

But when Jules had told Harry, he'd surprised everyone by proposing. Jules had flown into the café near Vannie's work, bursting to tell her the news. Vannie had nearly fallen over when she learned what had happened.

'Please tell me it's not true,' she'd said, her heart beating fast. It couldn't be true. It *couldn't*.

'It is!' Jules's face had been glowing, and she'd held her hand out where Vannie could see a small ring with a minuscule diamond. 'It's only a placeholder until he can take me shopping for a proper one,' she exclaimed. 'I can't wait. We're going to do this quickly, before I start to show too much.'

Vannie was frozen, still unable to believe this was happening. 'What does your father think?' she asked finally, picturing Thomas's handsome face creased with worry and concern that his only daughter had been knocked up so young. He did like Harry, though, and he would do anything to make Jules happy, especially after what had happened with her mother.

Jules shrugged. 'He was upset at first, but he's come around.'

'Jules...' Vannie drew in air. 'Are you... are you sure?' She was taking a risk – a huge risk, if Harry found out – by asking, but she had to. 'It's not too late, you know. I can take you to the clinic, and...' Her voice trailed off at the look on Jules's face.

'Take me to the clinic? Do you mean an abortion?' Her voice rose with every word. 'I'm not going to do that.' Jules put her hands in front of her as if she was protecting herself from Vannie, of all people. 'I don't need to do that. This baby is a part of me... and a part of Harry. I want us to be together now, to raise it together and to have a family – a happy family – again.'

Vannie dropped her head, pain twisting through her. She could understand that.

'Dad already has me looking at houses.' Jules's voice rang with excitement, and Vannie could see how much she had latched on to the idyllic vision of a future with Harry: the Harry she wanted him to be, the Harry she thought she had. If only she knew.

'But Jules, I—'

'Stop.' Jules put out a hand. 'I'm not going to listen to another word. I want you to be happy. You *should* be happy. I need to go.' She got up from the café where they'd been sitting, almost knocking over the chair in her haste.

Vannie stared as she hurried out, feeling as if she'd been stabbed a million times. She'd called Jules that night, over and over, but Jules hadn't answered. She hadn't responded the following day, or the next. Vannie hadn't been able to sleep or eat. Finally, she'd sent Jules a tiny pure-white BabyGro, trying to signal her support for the path her friend was about to embark on. If she wouldn't listen to Vannie, then Vannie would do all she could not to let this come between them.

Jules had got in touch at last, and Vannie had been there through thick and thin. She'd stayed by Jules's side, even when

Harry failed to materialise at prenatal appointments and almost disappeared once the baby was born.

Ivy had captured Vannie's heart, despite the fact that Vannie had never held a baby until she arrived. She was special, and the two of them had a bond that not even Jules understood. She connected with Ivy in a way no one else did, and instead of driving them apart, the baby brought her and Jules closer. Maybe, if Ivy was pregnant, this baby could bring them closer too?

But first she had to get Ivy. She had to make sure—

Shit! Vannie screamed as a branch crashed down from a tree overhead. She swerved, only narrowly missing it. The car skidded off the road, scraping with a terrible noise against the cement barrier on the shoulder.

'Christ.' She flicked on the hazards, then sat for a minute as the wind and the passing traffic buffeted the car before easing open the door. Her heart sank as she took in the bent rim of the front tyre. There was no way she was going anywhere with that. She got back in, chucking the mobile on the seat when she noticed there was no service. She'd have to wait for someone to show up to help her.

Everything will be fine, she told herself, repeating the words she'd said to Ellie earlier. Ivy was safe at the airport. Inside the cellar, Jules would be distant and cool with Frederick, as Vannie had advised. And no one knew the full truth, anyway.

It was all under control. There was no chance of anything unravelling.

For now.

THIRTEEN

JULES

Jules stared into the darkness, trying to understand. What did Frederick mean, what he'd done to her that night? He hadn't done anything to her... well, besides lying about how he felt and then leaving. Was he lying again? She sighed, thinking of how she'd planned to tell him to go. But now here they were. She couldn't tell him to go, and she couldn't get away. And while she couldn't stop him from speaking, she didn't have to believe a word he said.

Another huge clap of thunder boomed above them, and a curious trickling noise met her ears. What was that? Frederick flicked on his torch, and she gasped at the liquid streaming under the door, reaching halfway into the room already.

The water gleamed like an oil slick in the glow of the torch, coming closer and closer. It wouldn't take long until it reached them. They could sit on crates in the back of the cellar to keep dry, but at the rate the water was flowing into the room, the level could rise quickly. They could pile the crates, but... she looked up. The space down here was a good size – maybe the same as her lounge back home – but the ceiling was low. Still, it would need a fair bit of water to completely flood. And the locksmith should be coming soon. She dragged a crate further back into the cellar, away from the dark water spreading across the floor.

Frederick cleared his throat, and Jules braced herself for what she was sure would be more lies. 'That night... yes, I was drunk. OK, very drunk. You were too.' The words seeped towards her like the water. 'And maybe we should have waited to sleep together, but I never meant to hurt you. I'm so sorry if I did. I really did think you wanted to sleep with me. I never suspected in a million years that you didn't. I would have stopped, if that was the case. Please believe me.'

Jules jerked back as if she could dodge what he was saying. *Slept together?* But Vannie had said... Vannie had said nothing had happened. Jules had been so happy; so relieved. There was nothing to tell Harry. There was nothing to feel guilty about, besides one drunken kiss. She stared in the dark, her mind spinning. Could what he was saying be true? *Could* they have slept together?

No. She would have known. Wouldn't she? But she knew the answer. Of course she wouldn't have. She had been so drunk she'd barely even known where she was. She'd trusted Vannie's words when she'd awoken that morning, but now Frederick was telling her something different. More lies, she reminded herself. It had to be more lies.

'I was so happy that night. I loved you, Jules.' His voice caught. 'And I thought that finally, we could be together. I'd been waiting for that moment for ages. It felt like a dream.'

Jules breathed in, remembering his expression when she'd said that she was done with Harry... that she didn't want to be with him anymore. She needed a man who could be there for more than the good times. Frederick had shown her a different world was possible – a different *man* was possible – and she'd been so excited to go travelling with him. He'd opened her eyes.

'Our first kiss by the pool was magic,' he was saying. 'I know that sounds such a cliché, but it really felt so natural, so right. We drank all that champagne and when you asked me up to the bedroom, I knew I should say no – that we'd both had too much to be thinking clearly.' He let out a breath. 'But I was twenty-one. I was drunk, and I was in love. Not that any of that is an excuse, but I couldn't stop myself. I'd been waiting for so long.'

Jules swallowed, trying to grab on to the wavy images swimming through her brain. The lounger, pulling Frederick up, both of them laughing as they tried to navigate past the pool without falling in, Frederick taking her arm as they went up the stairs... she did remember that.

'Things do get a little blurry at that point, but I remember that we undressed and that we had sex. I thought you wanted it too. I remember falling asleep beside you.'

Jules's heart pounded as she listened to his words. *Was* he telling the truth? He sounded so genuine, but then he'd sounded the same that night, too, before leaving. She strained to make the darkness in her head flash bright, but still she remembered nothing.

'I woke up a couple of hours later with a splitting headache. I don't usually drink that much. You were still sleeping. I went to the bathroom to get some Nurofen. I was so drunk, it took ages to find it. When I came back...' He swallowed, and she could hear the pain in his voice.

'What?' The word emerged as a croak. She didn't want to hear more. She knew what he was saying couldn't be true. And yet... and yet something within her needed to hear him speak.

'When I came back, Vannie was leaving your room. Her face was unlike anything I'd ever seen before. Fierce. Staring at me like I was a criminal. Like I'd *hurt* you.' He drew in a shuddery breath. 'She wouldn't let me inside your room. She grabbed my arm and practically dragged me down the stairs. She told me that you said I'd...' He paused. 'That I'd forced myself on you. That you'd tried to stop me, and I wouldn't. She said you were in absolute bits, crying and shaking. She was *furious*.'

What? What the hell? Jules blinked, struggling to take in what Frederick was saying. Could that have actually happened? And she didn't remember any of it? She wanted to tell herself once more it was lies. But how could it be? Why would he lie about doing something so awful?

'I wanted to get back in to see you, but Vannie wouldn't let me. I tried to argue with her, but she made me doubt myself. I'd had so much to drink. Maybe I hadn't listened to you. Maybe I should have stopped.'

Jules was silent as his words swirled around her. She tried again to recall that night, but everything was still so fuzzy.

'Vannie told me to go. To go, that very moment, and if I ever saw you – if I ever dared to come near you – she would tell the police what had happened. She'd get you to say everything.' Frederick's voice cracked. 'And even though I didn't think I had done anything wrong, well... I had been drunk, and I doubted myself. I had to go. I had to leave.'

Jules stayed silent, swaying back and forth on the crate. Maybe... maybe she had told him to stop. Maybe, in his drunken state, he hadn't listened. Maybe he *had* done that to her. The very fact that he'd doubted himself – that he'd left – told her it could be possible, although she couldn't begin to imagine it.

'I got my things and called a cab. I went to the airport and flew to Paris, mucking around for a few days, trying to think of what I should do. I was so messed up, I felt like I didn't know myself. Like none of what I'd planned was for me now. It was for a different person.'

Jules nodded. She could understand that. Once she'd fallen pregnant, her old life had been behind her too.

'At a hostel, I met someone who was flying to Vietnam. I'd been planning to go a few weeks later, anyway, so I booked a ticket and went. I picked up odd jobs and eventually worked my way up to the guest house. My life became centred there, and I tried not to think about everything that had happened here. I tried not to think about you.'

Jules kept quiet, giving him the time and space to let the story unfold, despite the questions hammering into her. She couldn't believe this had happened. She couldn't remember any of it. If it *was* true, then why hadn't Vannie told her?

Maybe... Jules swallowed as the thought flooded in. Vannie knew how vulnerable Jules had been after the death of her mother. She knew she wouldn't be able to endure any more trauma. If she'd told her nothing happened, maybe it had been because she'd been trying to protect her, as always.

Even so, the idea that Vannie had kept something so huge from her – this awful, powerful thing – for so long made Jules feel uncomfortable as if she'd been sitting blissfully in a dark place when the reality was something different. Was she planning to keep it from Jules forever? She bit her lip. Was *this* why Vannie had been so upset when Frederick turned up? Because she'd been worried Jules would find out?

Perhaps she should be grateful, she told herself. Why would she want to know, anyway? It wouldn't have made any difference – well, besides making things a million times worse. Frederick was right. She was lucky to have Vannie as a friend.

'But of course I missed you,' Frederick was saying, 'and I hated myself... hated what I might have done to you. I couldn't really believe it, but I couldn't trust myself either. All I could do was stay away.'

'So, what changed?' Jules asked. 'Why did you come back? And to come here, with Vannie, in this place where it happened, well...'

'I know.' Frederick let out a low laugh. 'It's crazy, isn't it? To be honest, I wasn't sure I could do it until I actually got on that plane, and then until I got into the taxi. Pulling up to the villa and forcing myself to get out of the car was one of the hardest things I've ever done. Leaving here back then, leaving you and knowing what I'd done, was the hardest.'

Jules felt a tear drip down her cheek. Surprised, she swiped it away. Why was she crying?

'But, well, things change. And sometimes, what you thought was locked away isn't. Sometimes, you need to face it.' He shifted on the crate, and the wood creaked beneath him. 'When Ellie got in touch about the reunion, it seemed like the perfect chance to talk to you. I had to talk to you, no matter where it was. No matter how painful.'

She wiped her eyes, thinking she wasn't sure she'd do the same if she was Frederick. But then, he had always been the type to stand up, to face any fear. She remembered once, back in their second year, when a couple had been fighting on the street outside their house. It had been late, and the yelling had jolted them all awake. Despite Harry telling him to leave it, Frederick had gone outside and told the man to calm down, then asked the woman if she was OK. Frederick was tall, but the man was heavy-set, and when he swung at Frederick, he nearly knocked him off his feet. But Frederick didn't back down, and when Safet appeared beside him, the man turned tail. Jules had watched the action unfold from the lounge, secretly wishing Harry could be so brave. That's why she'd been so surprised when Frederick had disappeared. She'd thought it was so cowardly, and she'd believed he was anything but a coward.

'Because it's not just about you or me.' Frederick had continued speaking.

Jules tilted her head. What did he mean?

'There was something else,' he said. '*Someone* else. Someone who brought the past into the present.'

FOURTEEN

ELLIE

'Where on earth is Vannie?' Ellie paced back and forth across the flagstones in the kitchen, staring anxiously at the pouring rain. It was coming down so hard that the water in the pool was splashing up. And where was Safet, for that matter? 'It shouldn't take this long to drive to the village and try to hunt down a locksmith.'

Harry looked up from where he was sitting at the counter, rifling through a stack of papers. His leg was jiggling, and she could feel his nervous energy. He'd sworn when she'd told him Jules was trapped in the cellar, and even though she wasn't in danger, Ellie could see how desperately he wanted her safe and sound.

'Maybe she had to go even further,' he said. 'I can't imagine there are many locksmiths in that tiny place.' He got to his feet. 'I'm going to call the manager again. He needs to do something. This is ridiculous.'

'I'll call,' Ellie said quickly. She'd booked the place. She was the one in charge – or at least she was trying to be. She grabbed her phone, eyebrows rising when she noticed she had no service. Was that because of the storm? 'Does anyone have reception on their mobile?'

Her heart sank when Nicola picked up her phone, then put it down with a sigh of frustration.

'I don't have any either,' Harry said, glancing at his. 'Maybe one of those lightning strikes took out a tower, or maybe it's too weak right now. I'm going to head to the attic. Higher up, we might be able to pick up a signal.' He got to his feet.

Ellie was about to tell him to sit down – that she'd do it – when Safet came in.

'Oh!' She gasped as he came towards her. His face was pale and he was dripping wet, his dark hair plastered to his head. 'Where on earth have you been? I was worried sick!' She moved to hug him, momentarily forgetting what had pulled them apart in the first place.

Safet stepped away, and her heart dropped. 'I got caught out on one of the trails when the storm broke. There was nowhere to shelter that would be safe, so I came back here.' He swiped water from his face. 'The wind is brutal. Up on the hills it's bringing down trees. And the rain... I almost got swept away by a stream. It was tiny when I first crossed it, but it had doubled in size when I tried to get over it again. I wouldn't be surprised if there's some flash flooding in the valleys around here – there's not the capacity to drain this amount of water. You should see the back field out there. It's practically a lake.' He paused. 'Is everyone OK? Victoria? Ahmed, you all right?'

Ahmed nodded, moving closer to Ellie.

'Victoria and the twins are in the annex. But...' Ellie swallowed, almost not wanting to mention Jules's name. 'Frederick and Jules are trapped in the cellar out back. They went in there, the door closed, and the old lock engaged by accident. We don't have a key – I've talked to the manager, and he's trying to track down a locksmith. Vannie is too.'

Safet shook his head. 'I can't see anyone agreeing to come

here in this storm.' Panic flashed across his face. 'Did you say the cellar out back?' He pointed towards the pile of stones they could barely make out through the rain-streaked window.

Ellie nodded. 'Yes. Why?'

'You know how I said the field has turned into a lake?' He held her gaze. 'Well, when I passed by, I noticed the excess water was draining down the stairs and into the cellar. There's a ton of water on that field. If it keeps draining, Jules and Frederick could be at risk.'

At risk? A jolt of fear went through her, but she told herself to calm down. They'd get them out. She stared at her husband, trying to gauge his level of concern. Was it normal, like it would be for any friend? Or was it more, like it would be for someone he was intimate with; cared for as a lover? God, she hated that she was thinking this, now of all times. Anger pricked inside at both Safet and Jules. What on earth were they up to?

'Ellie?' Ahmed's voice was faint, and she glanced down to see him practically vibrating with fear. After being shut in there himself, this was the last thing that would help him relax. 'I'm scared. I—'

'Don't worry,' she said quickly, touching his shoulder. 'Vannie will be back any minute. They'll get out, and everything will be OK.' She drew in a breath, Jules's voice ringing in her mind, and pulled her husband to one side. 'Jules said you both wanted to talk to me about something. Can you...' She paused. 'Can you tell me what it is?'

Safet met her eyes with an expression she couldn't make out. But then, as well as she knew him – better than anyone – there were times he retreated into himself and she couldn't reach him. Like now, when he was right in front of her and she had absolutely no idea what he was thinking. Was he upset that she had practically accused him of having an affair? Or was he upset because he really was having an affair?

'Now's not the time,' he said, putting a hand on her arm. It should have felt comforting, but it was like a heavy weight. 'Let's talk when she's out. When everyone is safe.' He paused. 'They'll be fine in there for a little while, but it's probably not a big space. It won't take long to start to fill up.'

Just then, they heard a car pull up outside, and Ellie's heart lifted. 'Vannie!' Thank God. Now, they could get Jules out, and then they could all talk together.

But the woman who emerged from the car, shivering and pushing her wet hair out of her eyes, wasn't Vannie. It was... Ellie squinted for a second, trying to place her. It was Ivy, Jules's daughter. It had been years since Ellie had seen her. What was she doing here?

'I'm going to try to dig a trench to divert the water from the cellar,' Safet said. 'It might not work, but it's worth a try. I can't sit here doing nothing.' He disappeared before she could respond.

Ellie sighed, watching as Ivy dashed from the car that had dropped her off and towards the villa. Rain continued to pour down the windows, obscuring the view outside where Safet had gone to dig a trench, trying to direct the flow of water away from the cellar to save his precious Jules. Her mouth twisted. She didn't want to think like that, but she couldn't help it. Her hope of gaining the group's admiration had come to nothing, and the one thing she had been most proud of – her husband – might have been taken away by the person she was hoping to impress. It would almost be funny if there wasn't a chance it was true.

'Hello.' Ivy looked at Ellie tentatively. 'I hope it's all right that I've come. That I haven't put you out or anything. I... I really need to talk to Mum and Vannie.' She glanced around. 'Is Vannie here? I tried to call her mobile, but she's not picking up. I managed to get a ride from the airport, after all. I didn't want her to have to come all that way.'

Ellie raised her eyebrows. Had Vannie known Ivy was coming? Why hadn't she said? But maybe Ivy had called while she was out trying to find the keys, and then the mobiles had gone down. 'Of course it's OK that you're here!' she said. 'Your mum will be happy to see you.'

'I know. She always is. But...' Ivy let out a breath. 'I'm not sure she will be this time.' She looked so worried that Ellie squeezed her close. 'I really need to tell her something.'

'Whatever it is,' Ellie said, 'getting it off your chest can only be good.' She winced at the words, thinking of the secret she was holding close. It could have changed everything too. It still would, if she told Safet. She had no doubt of that.

'Right, so where's Mum?'

Ivy's voice jerked her back to the present, and Ellie bit her lip. How to explain?

'Well, you're not going to believe this.' Ellie forced a smile, trying to make light of it. 'There's a wine cellar across the back field. Your mum went in to have a look with a friend of ours, and the wind slammed the door shut. Somehow the old lock engaged, and we don't have the keys.'

Ivy's mouth dropped open. 'No! So she's stuck in a wine cellar?' She grinned. 'Only Mum.'

'Vannie's trying to find a locksmith. I'm sure she'll be back soon. In the meantime, Safet is out there making sure no water drains into it. Don't worry, they're not in danger. It's only to make sure they stay dry.' She didn't want to alarm Ivy.

'Don't tell her I'm here, OK?' Ivy swiped water from her face. 'She'll think something's wrong, and I don't want her to worry.'

Ellie nodded. 'All right.'

'Should we help?' Ivy asked, and Ellie glanced out the window to see that Harry had joined Safet in trying to divert the water. Ellie called to Ahmed that she was going outside for a bit, then followed Ivy to the field. Her heart sank as she took it in. Safet was right: it was like a lake, and the water was over her ankles. If this lot did drain into the cellar, then Jules and Frederick definitely would be in danger.

Harry jerked in surprise when he saw his daughter, then gave her a quick hug and handed her an extra shovel. Ellie grabbed the metal post that Safet had brought out from the shed and started digging alongside the others. A few minutes later, her breath was coming fast and every muscle in her back ached. But the water seemed to be diverted away from the cellar steps, cascading down the chute they'd created in the side of a small slope.

'God, people in London would pay through the nose to get a workout like this.' Ivy was panting and her face was red, and Ellie felt a sense of relief that at least she wasn't the only one finding this taxing. 'I—'

Safet's shout cut her off, and they looked up from the bottom of the slope to see a wave of sludge coming towards them. Ellie grabbed Ivy's arm and dragged her aside, heart sinking as the trench they'd been digging was completely obliterated by the mud. She gasped as she saw her husband lying on his side at the top of the slope, his face contorted in pain. As quickly as she could, she made her way up, the mud sucking at her feet with every step.

At last, chest heaving and legs burning, she was at her husband's side. 'Are you OK? What happened?'

He groaned as he looked up at her. 'I must have dug too deep and made the slope unstable, especially with all the mud. It started sliding, and I tried to jump out of the way. I twisted my ankle.' He tried to move but let out another cry of pain.

Panic lurched inside her. This was more than just a twisted ankle, she knew that much. Safet had a crazy-high pain tolerance – when he'd fractured his wrist after breaking up a fight between two young lads, he'd carried on at the refugee centre for hours despite it swelling.

'Stay still,' she said. 'Harry will get you inside to where it's dry, and then we can take a closer look.' She glanced up at Ivy, who was beside her now with a white face.

'What about Mum?' She pointed to where the water was cascading down the steps with even more force, her face tight with tension and worry. 'It's really getting in there. We have to do something.' She bit her lip. 'I wish I knew where Vannie was. I hope she's all right.' Ivy frowned and pushed her long blonde hair out of her face in a gesture so much like Jules, for a second it felt as if the years had rolled back and their younger versions were here again. 'I tried over and over to call her to say I'd managed to get a ride here, but she never picked up.'

'She'll be fine,' Ellie said, hoping it was true. 'It's just the mobile network that's down.' She touched Ivy's arm. She was freezing. 'Your mum will be OK too. We'll think of something to get her out of there, and she'll be thrilled that you're here. Let's help Harry get Safet inside, and then we'll find a solution to all of this.'

She prayed that, somehow, they would.

Before it was too late.

FIFTEEN
VANNIE

Vannie trudged down the long gravel track towards the villa, her body bent forward against the wind. She was lucky to have made it here intact after the one driver who'd stopped to help had refused to drive down the narrow track to drop her off, saying it was simply too dangerous. He'd implored her to stay at a nearby inn on the main road. But she couldn't, of course. She had to be there for Ivy and Jules, no matter what. Please, God, may Ivy still be safe and sound, waiting at the airport.

Vannie opened the door of the villa and walked into the lounge, every bit of her heavy with exhaustion. Her feet were blistered in their flimsy sandals and the linen shirt she'd thrown on earlier was plastered to her skin. But finally, she was here.

'Vannie! I tried to call to say I'd got a lift, after all, but I couldn't get through.'

Vannie blinked as Ivy threw herself into her arms. Was she hallucinating? How the hell had Ivy got to the villa? And... she cast a glance around, noticing Jules and Frederick were nowhere to be seen. They must still be in the cellar. At least she'd get the chance to talk to Ivy first, as Ivy had wanted.

'Did you find a locksmith?' Ellie's eyes were wide and anxious.

'No,' Vannie responded. 'I didn't even make it into the village. I swerved to avoid a falling branch, and my tyre rim got bent. I had to wait until someone came by to give me a lift. It took forever.' She grimaced as she peeled off the sandals. 'It's such a shame the weather isn't better for you, Ivy, but I'm sure Jules will be so happy to see you. *I'm* happy to see you.' She put a hand on Ivy's arm, stealing a glance at her mid-section to see if she was right that Ivy might be pregnant. She couldn't see anything, but of course it could be very early days. God, she couldn't begin to imagine Ivy with a baby, but then Jules had only been a couple of years older than her when she'd fallen pregnant.

'I can't believe Mum's stuck in the cellar. I hope she gets out of there soon.' Ivy's voice was trembling.

'I'm sure she'll be OK,' Vannie said, wincing as she thought of how long Jules had been trapped in there with Frederick. She *would* be OK, though. Vannie had helped her get through so much. She'd help her through whatever Frederick had told her too – if he'd said anything at all. 'She's safe and dry. She'll be fine until we get the key.'

'We can't wait. She's not safe and dry.' Ivy's tone was frantic. 'The cellar is filling up with floodwater from the field. You should see it all draining in!' Vannie raised her eyebrows. *What?* 'We tried to divert some of it by digging a trench, but the slope collapsed. Safet hurt his ankle.'

She gestured towards the lounge, and Vannie peered in to see Safet on the sofa. His foot hung at an awkward angle, resting on a pack of ice. God, this was going from bad to worse. But it wasn't Safet she was worried about.

'Harry and the girls are looking for the first-aid kit,' Ellie said.

Vannie nodded. A bandage and some ice were hardly going

to cut it, though. What he really needed was an ambulance, some good pain meds, and a proper brace to immobilise it.

'Did you manage to call emergency services before the mobiles went down? They need to take a look at his foot. And I'm sure the fire brigade or police could ram the door open.' It might not have been an emergency before, but if the cellar was flooding, it certainly was now.

But Ellie shook her head with a sombre look, and Vannie's heart dropped.

'Let me get changed, and then we can talk about what to do, OK?' She limped up the stairs to the bedroom. They had to get Jules out of there – fast. But what *could* they do? Try to bail out water? That wouldn't work with the sheer volume. Ram the door down themselves? Safet was out of action, but Harry might be up to the task. She grimaced, thinking how Harry would never let anything happen to Jules. He needed her too much.

'Oh, hey, babe. You're back. Took you long enough.' Nicola was sitting on the bed, running a brush through her hair. 'Did you find anyone to get the door open? Can we enjoy our holiday now?'

Vannie stared at her girlfriend, thinking how beautiful she was... how *young*. Vannie had relished her fresh, unsullied take on life at first; how she had no baggage weighing her down. Now, though, that seemed like more of a burden than a break.

None of this was fair on Nicola. She'd only wanted to come on a trip with her girlfriend. It wasn't unreasonable to expect to spend time with her. But Nicola could never understand the complex ties that bound them all together here, and Vannie could never explain.

'I didn't find anyone, no.' She crossed the room and sat down on the bed beside Nicola. 'I'm sorry. I know this isn't what you wanted.' She touched her leg. 'Safet's lying down there injured, and floodwater is pouring into the cellar. I hate to think it, but Jules and Frederick could be in danger if we don't get them out soon.' Her heart lurched at the thought. 'And now Ivy's here. She says she needs to talk to Jules, and to me. I have a feeling she might be pregnant. I don't know – something in her voice.' She swallowed. 'I don't want to put her under too much stress. I couldn't stand it if she was pregnant and something happened to the baby because she was so worried about her mum.'

She got up and sloughed off her wet clothes, tugging on capris and a T-shirt. 'There might be something lying around that we could ram the door with. Do you want to come with me to help?' She struggled to picture slender Nicola ramming a door. 'Or maybe you can keep Ivy company. Try to distract her, calm her down.'

Silence filled the room, and then Nicola crossed towards her. 'Vannie...' She bit her lip, looking out the window at the trees swaying and the rain lashing down. 'I need to tell you something.'

Nicola's tone made Vannie pause. What on earth was she going to say?

'I'm not proud of this,' she started. 'But...'

Vannie drew back. 'What? What have you done?'

Her voice was sharper than she'd intended, and Nicola's face hardened. Vannie took a breath, telling herself to calm down. Getting angry right now wouldn't help anything.

'I was upset,' Nicola said. 'I was hurt, and I wanted to get rid of her – just for a bit. Because it's always about her, isn't it? Whenever she's around, you don't see anyone else. It's like I don't exist.'

Irritation curled through Vannie, and she let out a breath. Not more rubbish about Jules. She didn't have time for this right now. Nicola really needed to get over herself. 'Nicola, I—'

'When I heard the two of them were stuck inside that cellar, I was happy,' Nicola said to cut her off. 'Finally, she was out of the way. Ellie said where the keys were, so I ducked out there and took them before she could get to them.'

'What?' Vannie drew back. '*You* have the keys? You've had them all of this time?'

Nicola shrugged, and Vannie could see she was trying to feign nonchalance even though her face was flushed.

'Yup.'

Vannie stared. 'We've been running around like chickens with our heads cut off. Safet even hurt himself digging a bloody trench! And you could have opened the door?' Anger and disbelief curdled her insides. Jules didn't need to be trapped inside with Frederick. She didn't need to be in danger. None of this needed to happen.

Nicola dropped her gaze. 'I didn't mean for Safet to get hurt, obviously. Or for them to be in real danger. I thought they'd be in there until the manager could get here and let them out. I didn't know there'd be a great big bloody storm, did I?' Her eyes glistened with tears. 'I know it was stupid. Of course it was. I should have said that I had the keys, but by then too much had happened to come clean. I thought I could wait until you got back with the locksmith.'

She shifted on the bed. 'But I don't want anyone else to get hurt. I don't want Jules and Frederick to be in danger. And Ivy...' She shook her head. 'I know how much you love her. I don't want any of this to impact her, whether she's pregnant or not.' She paused. 'I'm sorry. I didn't want this to be a repeat of every other time we're with Jules. You forget that I'm here, and I'm tired of competing with her.'

Vannie sighed, thinking once more that Nicola could never understand how much Jules meant to her. She was more than a friend. More than family, even. Jules was someone she knew would be there for her. Someone who had let her into her life, her family. Who had trusted her with the most precious thing of all: her daughter.

Someone she owed everything to.

No, Nicola could never compete with that.

'I'm sorry too,' she said. Now wasn't the time to begin to explain. Actually, she wasn't sure there was a time. Sadness filtered through as she realised she didn't *want* to share any of that with Nicola. She could never give her the love she needed – the depth of feeling she craved. 'Look, give me the keys, and let's get Jules out of there. Then we can spend the rest of the weekend together.' Maybe that would soften the blow when she broke up with Nicola when they got back to London.

'OK.' Nicola nodded.

Vannie breathed in. This would be over. Then she thought of Jules and Frederick, and tension shot through her again. *Hopefully* over, anyway.

'I hid them in there.' Nicola opened the drawer in the bedside table, lifted up some papers, and drew out the key ring. 'Can we say... maybe say that we found them somewhere? You know, not mention that I had them? I don't want everyone to be angry with me.'

Vannie nodded, thinking how awkward it would be if Nicola admitted to hiding them. At least she'd done the right thing in the end.

'Sure.' Her fingers closed around the key ring, and she took in another big breath as she felt her body relax. She'd unlock the door. She'd keep Jules safe once more.

Everything – and everyone – would be fine.

SIXTEEN
JULES

'What do you mean, someone brought the past into the present?' Jules asked Frederick, trying to understand. 'Who?' Could it be Vannie? Had she threatened to report the assault? She hadn't wanted him here, after all. Maybe she'd tried to get him to leave.

A long silence stretched, and Jules drew in a breath, wrinkling her nose at the scent of fetid water and damp. They were perched on the crates at the far end of the cellar. Piled two-high now, it kept their feet from the pooling water, but the level was quickly rising.

'Jules, the reason I came here...' Frederick paused. 'It was because I found out that I had a child, living in the UK.'

Jules froze. He had a child. A child, living in the UK. The words loomed large in the darkness.

'One of my friends bought me a DNA test ages ago, when they came to visit,' he said. 'A bit of fun, you know. Everyone was doing it. I found out my heritage, registered on the database, and promptly forgot about it.' He paused. 'But then, about two months ago, I got a notification of a new match – someone who could be my daughter.'

Oh God. *Oh God.* A daughter. Thoughts raced around her mind, but she couldn't grasp any of them. She didn't want to grasp any of them. All she could do was sit and wait, part of her dying to hear more and part of her wanting to close her ears to his voice.

'I was shocked, as you can imagine,' Frederick continued. 'I mean, I'd had a few relationships on and off over the years, some of them with British expats. But no one had ever told me about having a child.' She heard him let out a breath. 'Then I got a direct message through the site.'

Jules swallowed, her heart pounding. 'From whom?'

'It was from Ivy.'

Ivy. The thud of her pulse in her ears was so loud it was almost deafening.

'She told me who her mother was, and she said she wanted to meet. Ivy...' He paused. 'Ivy is our daughter.'

Our daughter. The words scrolled through her mind, over and over, in an endless loop. She couldn't take them in, though. And yet... somehow, she knew it was true. Somehow, it made sense. She *felt* it. Ivy was their daughter.

Jules gripped her arms so tightly her skin began to sting, but she didn't let go. She wanted to laugh, to cry, to shout. She'd been too drunk to remember she'd even slept with Frederick that night. Now, Frederick was telling her that not only had they slept together, but he'd assaulted her. And not only had he assaulted her, he'd got her pregnant.

He'd got her pregnant, and she hadn't known it was him. She never would have even suspected.

Had Vannie? Jules bit her lip, thinking she must have at least thought about it. Was that why she'd tried to persuade her to have an abortion? Why, when Harry had proposed, she'd tried to convince Jules to say no? Once more, discomfort circled inside that she'd had no clue about any of this. She'd been making such big decisions, and she hadn't known the half of it.

It was one thing to hide an assault, and another to hide the identity of her baby's father. Vannie should have told her.

Jules shifted on the crate, wondering what would have happened if she had. If she'd learned the baby was the result of an assault, would she still have had it? She breathed in, remembering how happy she'd been when she'd found out she was pregnant; how thrilled to learn of a new life in the midst of all the darkness. The truth would have killed her. It might have stopped her from having Ivy, the best thing in her life. In a way, she was grateful she hadn't known. That pregnancy had saved her.

'I couldn't believe it at first. I was shocked to think I'd got you pregnant... got you pregnant like that, but I could understand why you didn't want to tell me. If I had assaulted you, then of course you'd want nothing to do with me. I could hardly blame you.' He paused. 'But you don't even remember that night. This must be such a shock to you, Jules.'

Jules nodded, unable to speak. Shock was putting it mildly. 'So did Ivy...' Jules tried to get a grip on everything. 'Did you meet up?' Her voice was a squeak. How could all this have happened without her knowing? Why hadn't Ivy said anything?

'No. I wanted to talk to you first, so I didn't respond to her message. There's no way she can know who I am. I was registered under a username that isn't my real name.'

Jules dropped her head in relief. Thank God. She couldn't imagine Ivy going through all of that on her own.

'I'm so sorry, Jules.' Frederick let out a heavy sigh. 'For everything. It's a lot to take in.'

She nodded, thinking how that was an understatement. It *was* a lot, but Vannie had shielded her all of these years. Was she ever going to tell her the truth? And it wasn't only her she'd have to come clean with. It was Ivy too... and Harry.

Oh God. *Harry.* How would he react when he learned Ivy wasn't his child? He'd been so excited when he'd found out she was pregnant that he'd proposed. To discover the baby you thought was yours belonged to another man – another man who could have assaulted your wife, well... Jules couldn't imagine. She'd had to deal with finding out about the twins, and that had been hard enough.

She sighed, remembering the summer evening when she'd first found out. Ivy had been sleeping, and Harry had been out somewhere. A business trip, he'd said – he seemed to be away on one every week. But Jules hadn't minded. After five years married and three years together before that, Jules knew Harry was happiest when he was out and about, not cloistered away with her and Ivy. Besides, she loved the time alone with her daughter.

She'd been in the garden with a bottle of rosé and the ever-present baby monitor, enjoying the soft summer air and the way the light was slanting through the shadows. All of a sudden, a woman had been right in front of her.

She'd gasped. 'What are you doing? How did you get in here?'

'You left the door open,' the woman said, eyeing her with derision. 'So much for child safety, eh?'

Jules had sat up then, looking more closely at the woman. Hair so black it had to be dyed, thick black eyebrows and way too much make-up... she didn't look like the glossy, groomed women around here. Was she a drug addict hunting for money? Fear spurted through her.

'Look, whatever you want, I'll give it to you,' she said quickly. 'Then leave, OK?'

'I want to talk to you.' The woman's voice was intense.

'Me? Why?'

'It's about the babies, innit? The pram is inside there.' She jerked her head towards the house. 'Bloody double buggy wouldn't fit through the doors to bring it out here.'

Jules's brow furrowed. 'Do you need money, then? Is that

why you're here?' Maybe this woman was homeless or some-thing. She must be desperate if she was breaking into people's houses.

The woman laughed. 'Yeah, I need money, all right. I told him that I'd come see you if he didn't give me enough. Do you know how much these babies cost? One is bad enough, but two?' She glanced around. 'Where is he, anyway? Wouldn't answer my phone calls. I've been trying for weeks.'

Jules froze as she stared. This wasn't a random woman. These weren't random babies. She was talking... she was talking about Harry. The knowledge hit her in the gut like a punch. Harry had cheated. He'd cheated, and this was the result.

And it wasn't only the cheating. She'd wanted another baby – she'd been pushing for one since Ivy turned two. She'd thought Harry had been keen after angling for the big house, but he always put her off, saying their life was perfect; why add complications? And now she found out he had not just one child, but two with this woman?

'Twins,' the woman said, letting out a puff of air. 'Everyone said it would be a blessing, but right now it feels like a bloody curse.'

'How old are they?' Jules could barely speak.

'A few months,' the woman responded. 'He hasn't even been by to see them.' Her eyes filled with tears before she angrily swiped them away, and for an instant, Jules felt sorry for her. 'He made me promise not to tell you. He said he'd help, but he's barely giving me enough to feed one, not two. And so I'm here.'

'I'll give it to you,' she said quickly. Her first reaction was to agree to anything to make this go away... to make this woman and her babies go away so that Jules could do everything to carry on; to preserve her life.

'OK.' The woman's eyebrows rose as if she couldn't believe her luck.

Jules grabbed her phone. 'Text me your account details and I'll transfer a sum immediately. And... get in touch with me if you need anything, OK? Not Harry.'

'All right,' the woman said as she texted.

Jules breathed in the musty air now, thinking how the situation had unfolded nothing like she'd imagined. Marta had gone straight to Harry and told him what she'd done, almost shoving his face in the fact that his wife had agreed to give her money. Harry had come to her in tears, pleading for her forgiveness, telling her she was everything to him and that they couldn't throw it all away for one awful mistake. He'd begged her not to tell her father, saying he was a role model and he didn't want to lose his respect.

It was so rare for Harry to admit he *had* made a mistake that she knew how upset and afraid he was. But he was right: they couldn't let this ruin what they had. So she had forgiven him, trying her best to swallow back the hurt and betrayal. People did make mistakes; terrible ones that could lead to unspeakable tragedy. She knew that first-hand from her mother, and she wasn't going to let the same thing happen again. Her pain was worth less than keeping everything together, and so she'd done all she could to make their new blended family scenario as easy for everyone as possible.

She'd made the right choice back then, she knew that. Harry had bent over backwards to show how sorry he was. He'd never cheated again, and their life had remained smooth and unchanged ever since.

He'd want that to continue as much as she did, she thought, shoving aside the niggling doubt as she remembered how he'd wanted to sell the house. But he *did* relish the world they'd created, no matter what he was thinking at the moment. He wouldn't destroy it over something like this, just as she hadn't when he'd told her about the twins. It would be hard for him to accept that he wasn't Ivy's father, but it wasn't like Jules had cheated. For God's sake, she hadn't even known. Vannie could back her up on that.

Or... she tilted her head as a thought floated in. Maybe Harry didn't need to know. She could ask Frederick to keep things quiet; not to respond to Ivy's message. After what Vannie said he'd done that night, he didn't have any right to ask for more. And if what Vannie said was true, Jules couldn't bear telling Ivy how she'd been conceived. She could tell Ivy she'd been the result of a one-night stand – that much was true – and she'd lost contact with the father... also true. For all intents and purposes, Harry *was* Ivy's father. What difference would revealing the truth now make other than to hurt him? He'd kept the twins from her, after all. And if she'd had the choice, she had to admit she'd prefer not to have known. Perhaps keeping quiet was the best thing for everyone.

'Are you OK?' Frederick's voice was soft.

'I will be. I think.' She shifted again on the crates they'd stacked, the water touching her feet.

She would be OK. Ivy and Harry would be too.

Now, she had to get out of here.

SEVENTEEN
VANNIE

'Vannie? Can we talk?'

Vannie shoved the key ring under a pillow as Ivy stepped into the room. If they claimed to have found the keys now – with the guilt written all over Nicola's face – Ivy might suspect she had something to do with Jules being locked in. Vannie didn't want everyone to blame her girlfriend for what had happened. It was partly her fault, after all. She should have made more of an effort with Nicola.

'Of course,' she said. She'd talk to Ivy, then pretend she was looking for something – the first-aid kit Ellie had mentioned, maybe? – and 'accidentally' come across the keys. Ellie had said the water was rising, but right now Jules and Frederick were still fine. A few more minutes wouldn't make much difference. 'Come, sit,' she said, beckoning Ivy towards a little alcove with two cushioned chairs set in the bay window.

Outside, the wind was still whipping the trees back and forth, and the rain was running in panels down the window. Nicola eased out of the room after a quick hello to Ivy, looking only too happy to escape.

Ivy sank into a chair. 'Right. God. How to start? I've been

thinking about this so much, and now I have no clue where to begin.' She ran a hand through her hair, a nervous excitement tainting the air around her.

Vannie held her gaze, her excitement contagious as images of babies and bottles ran through her head. It would be hard for Ivy, of course. But Jules had done it, and it would be so nice to have a baby around again. An infant, gazing up at her adoringly...

'Right.' Ivy leaned forward. 'A couple of months ago, a friend gave me one of those ancestry kits. You know, where you can test your DNA and pinpoint exactly where you're from?'

Vannie's pulse picked up. So this *wasn't* about her being pregnant? She pushed aside the disappointment. It was for the best, of course. Ivy still had so much ahead of her. But where was she going with this? She tried to keep breathing, to stay calm as nerves shot through her. 'Yes,' she said slowly. 'They're supposed to be great fun.'

Ivy nodded. 'Well, I did one. I didn't expect anything shocking from the results. Mum always said her family was from Scotland, way back. And Dad had told me his had lived around Manchester.'

Vannie was quiet, waiting for Ivy to continue as the fear grew.

'And Mum's side did say that,' she said. 'But Dad's, well... that's where it started to get a little tricky.'

Vannie's heart was pounding now. 'Tricky? What do you mean?'

'The results said that Dad's side of the family wasn't from Manchester. Not even close,' Ivy continued. 'Which was fine. I thought maybe he was wrong, or maybe I'd heard wrong. He never talked much about his family. And you know I never met my grandmother, since she died when I was young.' She paused. 'But then I got a notification that I was matched with someone who could be my father. Someone... not Dad.' She let out a breath.

Vannie froze. No. This couldn't be happening. It *couldn't*.

Ivy's big blue eyes were wide. 'I reached out to him through the system. I told him who I was, and who my mother was.'

Vannie stayed still, trying her best to absorb every hit. Ivy had emailed her father – her real father. He knew he had a child. He knew he had Ivy.

Oh God. *Oh God.*

'But he didn't respond, and I had no other way to contact him. He'd taken the test a long time ago and was registered on the database, but he hadn't used his real name.'

Vannie sagged in relief. At least... she tried to grasp on to something to calm her racing pulse. At least Ivy didn't know who he was.

'And so I decided to talk to you... and Mum, of course. Because I want to know who he is. I need to know.' Tears came to her eyes, and she brushed them away. 'I've always felt out of place in our family. It's weird, but I've felt it. Close to Mum, yes, but Dad... As I got older, I told myself that was how Dad was. Not exactly paternal, putting it mildly. But then when I saw these results, it made sense. Finally. There was a reason I felt like that. Apparently, I have a ton of relatives in *Sweden*, of all places.' She paused once more, the sound of wind howling through the window filling the space.

'Did you know?' Ivy asked, her clear blue eyes meeting Vannie's. 'Did you know Harry isn't my father?'

Vannie held Ivy's gaze, her mind churning. She'd suspected it, right from the moment Jules had told her she was pregnant, a month or so after their trip to the villa. It was the reason she'd urged Jules to get an abortion; the reason she hadn't wanted Jules to marry Harry. Of course, there'd been no way to be sure, but she'd known very well it could be a possibility. And as Ivy had grown, her big blue eyes and striking Nordic features had made Vannie's suspicions even stronger.

And now, there was no uncertainty. Now, she knew for sure: Frederick was Ivy's father. And Frederick knew he had a child with Jules – a child who'd reached out to him.

Was that why he'd come? Why he'd braved talking to Jules again, despite what had happened that night? Was he telling her now, this very moment, that they had a child together?

A child who was here now?

God! She never should have let Ivy come in the first place. What had she been thinking? But Jules had had no idea, and she hadn't realised Frederick had either – or Ivy, for that matter. Now, they *all* could have, and soon.

A cold sweat broke over Vannie, and her chest tightened so much she could hardly breathe. This could ruin everything. Jules would know she'd lied when she'd told her nothing had happened that night; that Vannie had let her friend carry on believing her baby was Harry's when it could have been Frederick's. And Harry would be furious, feeling humiliated and duped that she might have known and hadn't said a word.

Would he tell Jules the secret she'd been trying to bury? The secret that had started this terrible chain of events?

She had to stop that happening. Not only for her, but for Jules too. She couldn't let Jules's world – the life she'd been so desperate to have after such tragedy – be torn apart once more.

'Did you know?' Ivy asked again. 'You must have. Mum wouldn't keep this from you. You know everything.'

Vannie's mind was racing. She had to do something. She had to say something to stop this spreading. But what? In all likelihood, Frederick would have told Jules about Ivy by now. It was too late to stop that, but maybe Vannie could explain to Jules that Frederick had said nothing happened between them, like she'd told her so long ago. He wouldn't want to tell Jules the real reason he'd left so quickly, would he? She'd say that she'd had no idea the baby could be his, and she'd urge Jules not to upset things now by telling Harry. Jules would listen to her, like she always did. And after all Frederick had put Jules through, he wouldn't want to risk conflict between Jules and Harry by revealing Ivy's paternity.

The only person she really needed to stop talking was in front of her now. If Ivy spoke to Jules and found out her real father was here at the villa, then Vannie was sure she wouldn't be able to hold her back from approaching Frederick. And how could she possibly hide it from Harry, then?

She had to stop Ivy from talking to her mother; from telling her what she'd found. But how?

An idea came into her mind, and she held it there for a minute. She bit her lip. It would keep Ivy quiet, yes. But...

'I did know,' Vannie started slowly, wondering if she was actually going to do this. But she had to. She had to so she could save everything else. 'I knew, but your mother didn't.'

'What?' Ivy drew back. 'How is that even possible?'

'Ivy, I need you to promise me that you won't talk to your mum about this, OK?' She held her breath until Ivy nodded slowly.

'OK.'

'But before I say anything, I want you to know that your mum loves you so much. So much.' She stared hard at Ivy as if she could drill that into her. 'She has never been anything but grateful to have you in her life. You know that, right?'

Ivy nodded, but her eyes looked worried. 'Vannie, you're scaring me. What the hell happened?'

Vannie's heart was beating fast, and she could feel sweat breaking out underneath her T-shirt. She didn't want to do this. She didn't want to hurt Ivy. But she had to. She had to or the pain of what might happen would be so much greater.

'Your mother was assaulted,' she said, reaching out to touch Ivy's arm as if that could cushion the blow. 'She was assaulted, and she became pregnant with you.'

Ivy's mouth fell open, and Vannie wanted to do all she could to take the words back as pain lurched inside of her. But she couldn't. She had to carry on.

'She...' Vannie paused, trying to conjure up the words. 'She doesn't remember any of it. It was after the death of her mother. She was drinking a lot at that time, and sometimes, she'd black out. It happened that night too.' She dropped her head, unable to bear the expression on Ivy's face. 'I saw her door open. It was still night and I knew she'd been drinking, so I went in. She told me she'd had sex, but that she didn't want to. I tried to ask with whom, but she passed out. And in the morning, she didn't remember anything.'

Vannie leaned forward on the chair. 'Maybe it was wrong not to tell her, but she was already in such a state that I didn't want to pile more on her. I mean, she didn't even remember. So I thought that would be it, and we'd all move on. But then... then she found out she was pregnant. But she was with Harry around the time of the attack too,' Vannie continued. 'So I was never sure, really, who your father was. And she was so, so happy.'

Silence fell between them, and Vannie held her breath. If only she could know what Ivy was thinking right now.

'Does... does Dad know? I mean, Harry?' Ivy's voice was a whisper. 'Does he have any idea?'

Vannie shook her head. 'No. He thinks you're his. He always has.'

The room went quiet again, the air heavy with the words Vannie had forced out.

'I won't say anything,' Ivy said, and Vannie could barely hold herself up as relief poured into her. 'I don't want to upset her. Her drinking is bad enough lately, and I can't imagine what this would do to her.'

'I think that's the right thing,' Vannie said. 'I can't imagine how hard it must be for you, but I'm so proud of you.' She put a hand on Ivy's arm. 'All of this is an enormous amount to take in. Are you OK?'

Ivy nodded. 'I think so.'

'We can talk at any time about it, all right? Any time.' Ivy nodded again. 'Look, why don't you go grab a glass of wine and relax?'

In the meantime, she'd go let out Jules and Frederick. She'd talk to Frederick and tell him the best thing he could do now was leave... that neither Jules nor Ivy wanted to see him after what they'd learned he'd done. If he cared about them, he'd stay away.

And as for Jules, she'd find out what Frederick had told her. If Jules did know that Frederick was Ivy's father, she'd urge her to keep it all under wraps until Ivy was older and more mature – that there was no need to upset her now. And if Frederick *had* told her about the assault, well... she'd think of something.

Vannie put a hand to her head, thinking she was the one who needed a drink. When would this end?

Soon, she told herself. It would be over soon.

She glanced at Ivy, who was still staring out the window, lost in thought.

'I feel sick at the thought that I reached out,' the young woman said. 'FreddoFrog. That was his username. Sounds so innocent, doesn't it?'

'Freddo Frog!' Ellie swept into the room. 'God, I haven't heard that for a while. Remember how we used to call Frederick that? He said he hated it, but I think he secretly loved it.'

The seconds seemed to slow as Ivy swung towards Ellie. 'Who did you call that again?'

Vannie wanted to move. She wanted to stop time; stop Ellie from answering. But she couldn't. She couldn't do anything.

'Frederick,' Ellie replied, smiling down at Ivy. 'Have you ever met him? Probably not; he went to Asia after our weekend here when we graduated. He was from Sweden, and your mum was great friends with him. I'm sure she could tell you some stories.'

'I'm sure she could,' Ivy said, sounding like she was gritting her teeth.

'He's here now. Ask him once he's out of the cellar. Hope he's keeping your mum good company.' Ellie smiled again, then went back down the stairs.

Silence fell once more, and Vannie's mind whirled. She tried to latch on to anything, but she couldn't. The silence pressed in against her, blocking every thought.

Ivy turned to face her with an incredulous look. 'It must be him, right? Frederick. The man Ellie was talking about. Freddo Frog. From *Sweden*.' The words streamed out of her. 'And *he's* the one in there with Mum now?' Her eyes were wild. 'Do you think she's all right? Do you think he's told her what happened? We have to get her out! Vannie, she can't be in there with him. Oh my God. Poor Mum.' Her face darkened. 'He must have told her, right? I mean, he knows about me. He must have said something to her.'

Her chest was heaving, and Vannie could see the anger coming off her in waves. 'And if Mum does know, well, she needs to understand that we're behind her all the way. It's not her fault. She shouldn't have to hide it; shouldn't be ashamed. Everyone should know what he did.'

Ivy got to her feet. 'I'm going to round up everyone and see if we can find something to break down that door.' And before Vannie could say a word, she went out of the room and clattered down the stairs.

Vannie's heart was pounding so hard she could barely catch

a breath. She couldn't let this happen. She couldn't let them out now. She couldn't let Harry find out about Ivy, or... She forced the fear back down. The secret *was* still locked away for the time being – thank God she hadn't mentioned the keys. She still had time to think... think of something.

She'd better think fast.

EIGHTEEN
ELLIE

Ellie paced back and forth in the lounge, her mind flitting between worry for Safet, then Jules, and then Frederick. Her husband was lying on the sofa, white and silent, his face contorted in pain. Even though they'd been searching the house, they still hadn't managed to uncover a first-aid kit. Ahmed was curled up in the corner, clutching his phone. Thank goodness he'd agreed to stop filming the girls, even if he'd seemed terrified at the thought of giving her the mobile. At the moment, she was glad he had it for a bit of comfort. This whole situation seemed to have made him even more anxious than usual, his big dark eyes glistening as if tears were about to fall.

'Is Safet going to be OK?' he asked.

She sank down beside him. 'Of course,' she said. 'He's a tough cookie, like you.' She smiled and stroked his hair, thinking he didn't realise how tough he was. Not many kids she knew could cross Europe on their own. Although he hadn't been alone, of course. He didn't talk about it much, but she knew he'd faced awful situations with traffickers along the way.

Her reassuring words didn't hit the mark, though, and Ahmed dug his fists into his eyes in a bid to stop tears from falling. Her heart dropped. She'd told him so many times it was OK to cry – that she wouldn't yell at him to stop or hit him, like others had done on his journey. But before she could say anything, he raced up the stairs. She sighed. Probably heading to the bathroom, where he'd lock the door and let out his emotions. She'd give him a few minutes before making sure he was all right.

Harry appeared, his face more anxious and drawn than she'd seen it before. All of this must be starting to get to him now. She'd witnessed last night how much he loved Jules, even if his over-the-top public displays of affection had annoyed her. And now Ivy was here, not to mention the twins. It must be hard to try to hold it together for them.

'Sorry, Ellie. I haven't been able to find bandages or anything.' He grabbed his phone. 'Still no signal.'

She bit her lip as a thought hit. What would *he* think of his wife exchanging so many messages with Safet? Would he believe there was nothing in it? Did he know? Was that behind all the fuss he was making over Jules last night at supper: to mark his territory?

Ellie let out a breath, picturing Safet's expression when she'd asked him about the texts. He hadn't denied it. But he'd given her that look as if somehow she'd wounded him... wounded their love and their trust. Then he'd disappeared into the woods, only to return and almost kill himself to get Jules out of danger.

Ellie shook her head in frustration. She didn't know what to think, but... her glance fell on his mobile on the coffee table across from him. If she could read those messages, she could judge whatever was going on for herself. All this had come about because of something Nicola had said. Maybe she'd got the wrong end of the stick. Maybe she shouldn't have been so quick to think there was something going on. She'd have a look and then she could move on.

She waited until Harry wandered from the room. Then, before she could stop herself, she reached out and entered the password on the mobile – Safet had never made a secret of it. Heart beating fast and with fingers trembling, she navigated to the message folder and clicked it open. One by one, texts from Jules scrolled down the screen, disappearing off it... more messages than Ellie had ever sent. Safet had never been one for texting, always preferring to talk rather than write. At least that's what he'd told her.

Heart in her mouth, she scrolled back towards the top and clicked one open.

Have you told her yet?

She dropped the phone, and it clattered onto the floor. Safet's eyelids fluttered, then lifted. Oh God. Told her? Told her *what*?

'It's OK,' she said, her voice high and shrill. 'Just dropped something. Close your eyes again. Try to rest.' She picked up the mobile as if it was a grenade. She didn't want to see more. She wasn't sure she could see more. But she had to. She had to know for sure. She drew in a breath and opened his response.

Not yet. Soon. I don't want to make this trip she's been looking forward to all about that. I want to talk to you first, anyway. Review all the specs on your tracing service and fix your start date together.

Ellie blinked and sank into a chair in relief, letting out a little laugh. Jules was going to start working for the centre – some kind of tracing service, by the looks of things. That's what this had been about. Safet had aired the idea over the years, saying it would be good to help refugees find any missing family members when they could get some extra funding. And Jules was the perfect person: she'd volunteered with the centre a few times over the years, and she could afford to work for next to nothing. It made sense that Jules would approach Safet first, given he was the executive director and oversaw the budget and staffing. God, what an idiot she was to worry. Of course Safet wouldn't have an affair. How could she have even thought that? He was as honest as they came.

She was about to put the phone down when Safet's last message caught her eye.

I'm still trying to digest it all myself. I wish I'd known. Look forward to hearing whatever else it is you have to tell me.

Ellie stared, so many thoughts running through her head that she could barely breathe. What had she read? *I wish I'd known.* She bit her lip. Known what? What did he have to digest? Something Jules knew too. Something... she swallowed. Something not simply about Jules working with them.

An image of that summer afternoon came into her mind, the dark-eyed woman and her note, and panic spilled into her. It couldn't be that. It couldn't be. But... She jerked as she thought of Jules's relative tracing service. Had Safet found out she'd lied? That he hadn't been alone, like he'd thought?

She sighed, thinking of how she'd regretted what she'd done. She'd tried to push it from her mind, but it had tortured her. So, a month before they'd married she'd decided she would come clean. Safet loved her – he wouldn't leave her, like she'd feared – and she didn't want to pledge herself to her husband knowing what she'd done. And this, well... giving her husband a member of his family back would be the best gift ever.

Heart pounding, she'd rung the hospital the woman had told her was treating Safet's cousin. Excitement circled inside as she waited for them to pick up the phone. Finally, she could get this off her chest. Finally, she could do the right thing. But when they answered and she managed to get across to someone who she was looking for – she'd never forgotten his name – they'd told her that Amir had died two months earlier. She'd hung up, sitting frozen in the chair. His cousin was dead, but Safet had had a chance to see him. A chance she had stopped because she was worried he'd leave her. And now, it was too late.

She'd realised then she could never tell him what had happened.

Could Jules have somehow found out that Safet had had a cousin who'd still been alive when he'd left for England? Did he know about the woman Ellie had talked to? And that Ellie had known all along? Was that why Safet had been so preoccupied; so distant lately?

No. She jammed a fist in her mouth to stop the cry from emerging, then set the phone down on the coffee table again and took a deep breath. Maybe Safet had found out he'd had a cousin still alive, but he couldn't have heard that she'd hidden it from him. If he had, then Ellie knew he would never forgive her.

But... Horror gripped her insides as the message scrolled through her mind's eye. *Look forward to hearing whatever else it is you have to tell me.*

What else did Jules have to say? *Was* it about the woman? Was she about to blow Ellie's marriage apart? Maybe that was why she'd been so desperate to talk. Maybe Jules had wanted to warn her.

God, she'd almost prefer it to have been an affair. At least then she could forgive Safet and they could move on. But this... this was worse. Because if he ever found out what she'd done, then she knew it would be the end.

She bent forward, her head pounding. Suddenly, she wasn't so keen to get Jules out of there. Whatever she knew, it would be much, much easier if it stayed locked away forever.

If only that were possible.

Jules swallowed, trying to keep the fear at bay as the water swirled around her legs. Thankfully, it wasn't too cold – the recent hot weather had warmed the streams and ponds – but Jules shuddered to think what was in it. At least it was dark so they didn't have to see any foreign objects floating in the murk.

She and Frederick were perched on two crates now, yet the water was still up to their shins. It kept coming and coming, and soon there would be nowhere high enough to escape it. It felt like hours since anyone had come to check on them or even tell them what was happening. With no mobile phone and no connection to the outside world, they had no idea whether the storm was still raging or if the locksmith was on his way. It felt as if they were the only two people in the world.

A loud thud on the door made her jump. 'What was that?' she asked as it came again.

'It sounds like they're trying to break down the door,' Frederick said as he got to his feet and sloshed through the water.

The noise came again and again, over and over, the sound almost deafening.

'Mum?'

The voice was so faint Jules could barely hear it, and for a second, she thought she was hallucinating. Was that Ivy? Had she somehow conjured up her daughter?

'Mum, are you OK? Please say you're all right.'

Jules could hear the fear and tension in her daughter's tone, and her gut wrenched. What was she doing here?

'Ivy.' Jules jumped from the crate and pushed through the waist-high water towards the door, leaning as close as she could to it. God, she wished she could break it down and gather her daughter in her arms. 'I'm fine, sweetie. What are you doing here?' She hoped everything was OK; it wasn't like her daughter to act on a whim. 'Don't worry. I'm going to get out of here.' Please God, may she get out of here. 'It will be all right.'

'Are you sure you're OK?' Ivy's voice was still worried. 'No one...' She paused. 'No one has hurt you or anything?'

Jules breathed in. She could almost feel Frederick's eyes on her in the dark. Ivy must know that Frederick was in here with her. She must have talked to Vannie, the only person who could have suspected who her father might be; the only person who could have confirmed it to Ivy. And... Jules swallowed. Vannie must have told her about the assault. Her heart dropped as she imagined her daughter learning she'd been conceived like that. What must she be going through? Jules would give anything to gather her in her arms and tell her how much she was wanted.

She bit her lip. Vannie would have done that, of course, but... *why* would she have even told Ivy about the assault? That wasn't something she needed to know. And surely it wasn't her place to say anything. So, why the hell would she?

The discomfort she'd felt at having so much kept from her ballooned into anger. Vannie might have been protecting her, but she'd also taken away her chance to deal with everything on her terms; to make decisions based on truth and not delusion. Vannie had been the one to tell her daughter who her father really was, not Jules. And Vannie had chosen to tell Ivy something Jules knew her daughter would never, ever get over. Whatever Vannie's reasons, she'd had no right.

'All's good here, I promise. I'm absolutely fine.' She didn't want Ivy to worry. Beside her, she could feel Frederick relax slightly, and empathy stirred inside. Maybe he didn't deserve to meet a daughter resulting from assault, but it must be painful to come face to face with the consequences of such terrible actions.

'Mum, we've been trying to break down the door with an old axe,' Ivy was saying. 'But the blade is dull, and the door is too thick. We can't get it open.' She sounded close to tears.

Jules sighed, wishing the strength of her love could open it up.

'Mobiles are down because of the storm, but as soon as we can, we'll call the fire brigade and get you out. Hang in there, OK? I love you,' Ivy called.

'I love you too.' Jules tried to put as much of that as she could into her voice.

Silence fell, and she sloshed back through the water and clambered up onto the crates.

'Vannie must have told her I'm her father. And that I assaulted you,' Frederick said, echoing Jules's earlier thoughts. 'She must have, for Ivy to say those things.' His voice was shaking. 'I understand her wanting to protect you. Not telling you the truth about that night, whatever she thought it was. She went too far once you found out you were pregnant, though. She should have told you then, but I can kind of understand.' He let out a breath. 'But why the hell would she tell Ivy? Why would she want her to know such a terrible thing?'

Jules could feel the anger rolling off him.

'I wish that night was clearer.' He paused, his desperation swirling in the air. 'What I did ruined my life. If you'd known, it could have ruined yours too. And it ruined us; any life we might have had together. I've lived with that ever since, and I can't even recall what Vannie says happened. It seems so... unreal, somehow. I want to understand how I could do something like that, but if I can't remember, I never will.' He sighed, the only sound the trickling of water.

'And sometimes I can't help but wonder... if there's any chance Vannie might have misheard you... that she might have got the wrong end of the stick?' He breathed out. 'I don't want you to think I'm trying to dodge responsibility. If I did hurt you, I deserve all of this and so much more. It's, well, I've thought about it over and over. I remember having sex. But I simply can't remember you asking me to stop.'

Jules blinked, once more trying to make that night clear in her mind. She could remember going up to her room. She could remember the feeling of wanting Frederick. She just couldn't remember anything beyond that.

'I suppose it's possible.' Had she been crying, maybe, when Vannie had come in? Sometimes, when she drank, she got very emotional. She'd really wanted to be with Frederick, after all. Could Vannie have thought that signalled Frederick hurting her, instead of the opposite? Vannie had always been very quick to jump in and protect her, Jules thought. Maybe she *had* jumped to the wrong conclusion. In a way, that was almost more believable than Frederick harming her.

Frederick's words about the life they might have had together drifted into her mind, and even though it was already so black inside, Jules closed her eyes as a million memories ran through her head. How they'd talked for hours in the lounge at home, the walks by the river, lying in the park, spinning stories about their future even though Frederick knew she was with Harry. She was with Harry, but somehow, the more time she spent with Frederick, the more she longed for something different.

They'd spoken over and over about travelling through Europe and then Asia after graduation, and how they'd settle down on a beach somewhere in a cheap-as-chips place, open a guest house and spend the rest of their days in a freedom they'd never experienced. Frederick had asked how many kids she wanted, and even though she'd never really thought about it, instantly, she'd said two. Frederick had nodded, telling her that although it seemed miles off and there was a lot he wanted to do first, he would love to have a family one day. His parents had given him the best childhood possible in rural Sweden, and he wanted to give his kids something similar.

It had sounded like a dream. It *was* a dream, Jules knew. Until that day in the villa, when she'd decided it didn't have to be. That it could be real. Until Frederick had abandoned it all.

But now she knew he hadn't left because he'd decided he didn't want her. He'd left because of something he'd thought he'd done to her... something that may not have even happened; something only Vannie remembered. Something Vannie had kept from her, but had told Ivy. Had she sworn her daughter to secrecy too? Tried to keep it once more from Jules? The thought made anger grip her again. Vannie may have protected her, but she could have destroyed Ivy in the process.

And *had* it really happened the way Vannie believed?

Vannie might not have all the answers, but right now Jules couldn't help feeling that, once more, her friend held the cards. Once more, Jules was in the dark. And while she might have needed that twenty years ago, she didn't any longer.

She had to talk to Vannie.

'Ivy!' Vannie ran across the sodden field, desperate to pull her god-daughter away from the cellar door she was striking with what looked like an axe. She couldn't open that door. Not until everything was under control. If only she could find a quiet place amidst this chaos and *think* about what to do. Maybe when Ivy calmed down, she could convince her once more to keep quiet. She simply needed time.

Ivy came up the cellar stairs slowly and dropped the axe on the ground. 'It wouldn't budge,' she said, her chest heaving as she tried to catch her breath. 'Do you think Harry might be able to break it down?'

Vannie held her gaze, her mind racing. 'He might, but it's not a good idea. If you open the door now, you could be letting in a rush of floodwater. It might be better to wait a little bit until we can stem the flow into the cellar, or the storm lets up.' She had no idea what she was talking about, but it sounded plausible. 'I know what you found out is upsetting, but we don't want to make things worse for them.'

'OK.' Ivy nodded, and relief rushed through Vannie that she seemed to have bought it. 'Mum seems all right for now, anyway.' Ivy caught sight of Vannie's face. 'Don't worry. I didn't say anything. I wouldn't in front of him.'

Thank God. 'Come.' Vannie put a hand on her arm and was about to usher her back into the house when Nicola appeared at her side.

'Where are you going?' she asked. 'Aren't you going to let them out?'

Vannie's heart dropped. Not now. 'Well, Ivy tried,' she said, hoping Nicola would misunderstand her. 'But she couldn't do it.'

'The keys don't work?'

Ivy stopped. 'The keys? What do you mean?'

Oh, shit. Vannie tried to think of something to say to stop this conversation from happening, but she couldn't come up with anything.

'You know. The keys... that Vannie found.' Nicola's eyes were darting from Ivy to Vannie and back again. 'The ones to get your mum out. I really hope you weren't too worried, Ivy. I hope the baby is OK.'

Ivy was turning to Vannie with a confused expression. Vannie's pulse raced. Damn Nicola! Why couldn't she keep her mouth shut?

'Vannie, what does she mean? You found the keys?' She tilted her head. 'And what baby?'

Vannie shot Nicola a look of death, praying she'd get the hint and stay quiet. 'I'm so sorry, Ivy. Nicola... well, she must have been drinking. I don't know what she's talking about, but I haven't found any keys. When she has too much, sometimes she gets a little confused.' Nicola was going to *kill* her, she thought. But she'd been planning to end it, anyway. Thank God she'd mentioned something about a baby that seemed completely nonsensical. Ivy might believe she was drunk – or something.

Nicola was shaking her head. With the rain streaming down her pale skin and her dark hair plastered to her head, she did look almost mad. 'Why are you doing this? You know I haven't been drinking. You know there are keys. You put them back in the drawer by the bed when Ivy came into the room.'

Vannie's heart lurched. *Shit*. At least she'd put them somewhere else, but if Ivy believed there were keys somewhere, she'd leave no stone unturned to find them.

'Ivy, Nicola's spouting nonsense,' she said. 'If I had the keys, I'd use them. You know I wouldn't want to keep Jules in there with him.'

Ivy stiffened, and Vannie could see her words had hit the mark.

'I know. I don't think you have them. You'd never do that to Mum.' Ivy bit her lip. 'But is it possible... possible Nicola *did* see the keys? Maybe they are in the drawer for some reason. Maybe the cleaners put them there by accident. Who knows? They might not be the right ones, but I couldn't live with myself if I didn't check.'

She started towards the villa, with Nicola and Vannie in tow. Nicola's face was like concrete, and Vannie could only imagine what she might be thinking. But she couldn't waste time on her. She had to think of what to say if they found the keys. Of what to *do* if they found the keys. She couldn't let Jules and Frederick out. Not before she came up with something to contain this whole thing.

They all marched into the bedroom, and Vannie pushed in front of them and over to the bedside table.

'Is this where you saw them?' she asked Nicola, trying to keep her voice as disbelieving and incredulous as she could, even as her heart was pounding. She opened the drawer as slowly as possible, attempting to buy herself time. Her brain seemed to be working in slow motion, unable to cope with all the moving parts. 'Surprise, surprise. There aren't any keys,' she said, as her pulse raced. 'Of course there aren't.'

'What?' Nicola rushed over. 'What do you mean? They

must be there! I saw you put them in there!' She yanked the drawer out and put it on the bed, rifling through its contents with wild eyes. 'Where are they?' She turned to Vannie. 'Do you have them? Did you put them somewhere else? You must have. Where?'

'What's going on?' Ellie appeared at the door of the room.

'Nicola thought she found the keys to open the cellar door,' Ivy said. She spun to face Nicola. 'Try to remember. Are you sure you saw them? Saw them here? My mum is in danger. *Please.*' Her face was white and strained.

Guilt poured into Vannie. What had she done? She put a hand on Ivy's arm. 'Ivy, I'm so sorry, but I really don't think there were any keys in the first place. Like I said, when Nicola drinks, she—'

'There were keys.' Nicola stood stiff and still like a soldier, defending herself. 'I'm not making it up. I know, because I took them in the first place. The cleaners never had them. It was *me.*'

Vannie sucked in air, the sound of her pulse thudding in her ears. Nicola must be furious at her lies if she was willing to admit what she'd done.

'I gave them to Vannie to open the door because I didn't want anyone to know what I did. I don't know why she's denying it. And making up all this bullshit about me.' Nicola pushed her hair behind her ears. 'I'm so sorry, Ivy. It was rubbish of me to keep Jules and Frederick in there. I just wanted some time alone with Vannie.' She turned to face her. 'But don't worry about that, Vannie. You're the last person I want to be with now.' Fury was pouring off her. 'As soon as the storm is over, I'm going back to London. I don't want to talk to you ever again.' She turned to Ivy. 'I hope you find the keys. And I hope your mum gets out.' And with that, she left the room.

Vannie watched her go. 'Wow,' she said, raising her eyebrows and hoping she looked shocked at Nicola's admission.

'I had no idea about any of this. I mean, I knew she was jealous, but... I didn't think she was capable of something like this.'

'So there *are* keys,' Ivy said slowly. 'But Nicola says she doesn't have them. They're not in the drawer, where she said you put them.' She met Vannie's eyes. 'Why would she say you had them?'

'I really don't know,' Vannie responded. 'But if she's angry enough to keep Jules locked in the cellar, then she's angry enough to lie about me – to try to ruin this whole trip with my friends.' She held her breath, hoping Ivy wouldn't probe more.

'OK.' Ivy nodded. 'You don't have them, obviously. So, where the hell are they?' She searched Vannie and Ellie's faces frantically as if they could give an answer.

The sound of a phone bleeping came from under the bed, like the battery was dying, and Vannie jerked. What was that? Had someone dropped their mobile?

Ellie bent to look under the heavy wooden bedframe. 'Ahmed!' she said. 'What are you doing here?'

Vannie glanced down as Ellie helped him out, an idea bursting into her head. It might not work, but at least it would give her some time. 'Maybe Ahmed has the keys. Maybe he saw where Nicola put them, and he took them.'

Ahmed stiffened, fear crossing his face.

'I'm sure he means no harm,' Vannie continued. 'He probably thought it was a game or something. Why would he be hiding here otherwise?'

'He was upset because Safet got hurt,' Ellie explained quickly. 'When he gets like that, he doesn't want anyone to see him. Perhaps he thought no one would look for him here.' Ellie glanced at him. 'Ahmed? Is that right?' But he kept staring at Vannie, his big dark eyes piercing almost straight through her. She reached out to take his arm, but he shrank away from her.

'Look, we're not going to hurt you or anything,' she said, trying to keep her voice calm. This kid was as jittery as she'd ever seen, not that she could blame him after all he'd been through. She didn't want to scare him even more, but she was fighting for her life now – for the people she loved most in her life.

'But we really need those keys.' Ivy's voice shook, she was so tense. 'Listen, you're not going to be in trouble. You probably don't even know those are the keys to open the cellar door.'

Ivy waited for him to answer, but he didn't move. He was like an animal caught in the headlights.

'But they are, and we need them. The water is rising, and we need to get them out. If we don't, well, they might die. And I don't want my mum to die. I need her.' Ivy's voice broke, and despite everything, Vannie felt tears come to her eyes too. 'Please, Ahmed. Please give me the keys.'

But Ahmed stayed frozen, and Ellie put a hand on his shoulder. 'He doesn't have them.'

'Maybe not, but can you be sure?' Vannie asked. 'Could you live with yourself if he did have the keys, and you didn't even check?' She could see by Ellie's face that she'd hit home with that one. Ellie was always so uncertain about things that it didn't take much to tip her over.

Ellie crouched in front of Ahmed. 'Don't worry – we're not angry with you. You won't be in any trouble. But if you have these keys, you need to give them back to us. Jules and Frederick are in real danger. We don't want anything bad to happen to them, do we?'

Vannie held her breath as they all waited for the boy's answer, but he remained silent.

'Let's check his pockets,' Ivy said. 'Then we can see for sure if he has them or not.' She stepped closer. 'Ahmed, can you turn your pockets inside out? Or let your mum have a look?'

But Ahmed put his arms around himself and shook his head furiously. Vannie stared, hoping he'd continue to resist. If she could stretch this out, it would only be a good thing. Now, if she could only *think*!

'Please, Ahmed.' Ellie's tone was pleading. 'Just show us.'

'We don't have time for this.' Ivy's face was a mixture of fear and determination, and she took Ahmed's arm and tried to pull him towards her.

But Ahmed wrenched away and, before any of them could move, he streaked from the room, his footsteps pattering on the stairs.

They stood there, the rain and the wind battering the window as Vannie tried her best to hide her relief. This was perfect. The longer it took, the more time she had to try to come up with a solution. Jules and Frederick should be OK for a little while.

'He definitely has those keys,' she said. 'And we're going to search this place until we find him.'

It could take an absolute *age*.

TWENTY-ONE
ELLIE

Ellie stared at Vannie, her heart sinking as Ahmed's footsteps faded away. She could only imagine how scared he was. Accusations of something so awful; threats to be searched... Ellie clenched her jaw. She knew he didn't have the keys. His silence was only because of his terror. He had been under the bed, but he hadn't been sneaking around. He loved hiding; loved anywhere dark. He was trying to stay safe from the trauma and fear that lingered. He hadn't wanted to show them his pockets, not because he'd had the keys, but because it would have reminded him of the times he had been searched... brutally, in some cases. That's why he had run.

She knew all of this. So why hadn't she protected him? Why hadn't she stepped up? Vannie had been so forceful, and Ivy so panicked. She'd let their emotions overpower her. In an effort to make them feel better, she'd let them traumatise her child. Hadn't she learned not to try to appease them by now? That her family was the only thing that mattered? Guilt poured through her as she pictured Ahmed's frozen face.

'Let's split up,' Vannie said. 'It will be faster. The sooner we find him, the better.'

'No.' The word burst from Ellie, and she moved to stand in Vannie and Ivy's way. 'Look, I know he doesn't have the keys. He only ran because he was terrified.' Maybe she hadn't protected him then, but she was going to now. She couldn't let them go on a witch hunt for Ahmed. He'd been through enough.

'Oh, really?' Vannie raised her eyebrows. 'How do you know that? How can you be so sure he doesn't have them?' She tilted her head. 'Do *you* have them?'

'Don't be ridiculous,' Ellie sputtered. 'Of course I don't.' What on earth was wrong with Vannie?

'What's going on?'

Ellie turned to see Victoria and the twins in the doorway. Worry was etched on their faces, even though the twins usually tried to play it cool.

'Girls, we need your help.' Vannie's tone was brisk and efficient. 'There are keys to get Jules and Frederick out, after all. But Ahmed has them, and he's run off. We need to find him.'

'Ellie, please.' Ivy took her arm. 'We need you. He might not come out for us, but he will for you. I can't let Mum die.'

She could feel all eyes on her. 'Ahmed says he doesn't have the keys. And I believe him.' She paused. 'It's no good chasing after him, trying to find him. It will only upset him more.'

Victoria scowled. 'Of course you would believe him, Mum. You'd rather let your friends die than think Ahmed could do something bad.' Her eyes filled with tears as she faced Ellie.

Ellie's heart lurched. How had things got to this point? How had she not known Victoria was hurting so much?

'I bet he does have the keys. He really is that messed up.' Tears were streaming down Victoria's face, and she angrily swiped them away. 'Please say we won't adopt him. There are other families who could take him, right? Please.'

She met her daughter's eyes, every bit of her wanting to engulf Victoria in her arms and tell her how sorry she was. Not only about this weekend, but that she hadn't noticed something sooner. She shook her head, thinking how much her daughter must not want Ahmed with them if she was saying this. Because as much as Ellie hated to think it, given what she'd learned about Victoria's true feelings this weekend, it was obvious she'd grasp at anything to get Ahmed in trouble.

'So, who are you going to believe?' Vannie's voice cut into her thoughts. 'Everyone else? Your own daughter? Or a psychologically damaged boy you've only known for a short time?'

Ellie blinked, feeling Victoria watching her keenly as frustration and panic swept over her. She didn't know what to do. She didn't know what to say. To Safet, to Jules, to her daughter... or even to Ahmed. She couldn't believe he had the keys. If she said that, though, it would look like she was dismissing her daughter in front of everyone. But she didn't want to traumatise Ahmed any more either. If only she had stuck up for him when she should have.

'OK.' Her voice emerged as a croak. 'If we split up and take a section of the villa to search, I'm sure we can find him quickly. Girls, you do this level. Vannie can take the attic and the ground floor. I'll look in the basement.' She knew Ahmed best. He loved anywhere dark, where he could hide. He must be in the basement.

And if she could get to him first, then maybe she could make this easier for everyone.

TWENTY-TWO

'How much longer do you think it's going to be?' Jules shivered in the damp and cold of the dark cellar. She realised Frederick had no way of knowing – knowing if they'd even get out alive – but she needed someone to give her hope. They didn't know if the storm had stopped, although water was still pouring in. It was up to their waists now, despite the extra height of the crates. They could stand on top of them if they had to, but with the low ceiling, they'd have to hunch over. She didn't want to think how low that ceiling actually was.

She sighed, thinking how ironic it was that she was turning to Frederick for hope. All of these years, she'd cursed him for leaving; for closing a door in her face. And now, trapped in this place with the water rapidly rising, knowing Frederick hadn't left willingly – that he hadn't rejected her, without saying goodbye – let a slice of light in, even with so much else still shrouded in darkness. Because she couldn't believe he would hurt her. She simply couldn't. Something had gone wrong that night, but it hadn't been between her and Frederick. She couldn't wait to talk to Vannie to find out more.

'I'm not sure,' Frederick responded. 'We could always crack

open one of those bottles of wine. Wonder how long they've been here.'

'God knows.' Jules rubbed her arms, feeling that same urge to drink sweep over her. Drinking had been her safety net through the years, enabling a filmy oblivion so she could float over the top of her life. She paused at the thought. Was her life really so bad that she needed booze to bear it? Didn't she get what she'd wanted when she'd married Harry? Beautiful daughter, successful husband, luxurious house... she should be happy.

Was she? The question weaved into her, and she held it there for a minute, letting her brain work at it instead of pushing it away. She was, mostly. It was simply that sometimes, she wanted *more*. More of what, exactly, she didn't know. That's what all of that business with Safet was about. It was easier to keep moving, to keep busy, than to stop and ask herself why she felt like that.

Jules's stomach let out a loud rumble, and Frederick laughed. 'Hungry? Wish I could fix you something. I make a mean omelette.'

Jules smiled. 'I remember,' she said, despite herself.

She'd never tasted anything as good as one of Frederick's omelettes. He'd made them for the whole group that first morning they'd woken up in the halls, too late to hit breakfast at the dining hall. They'd slumped over at the table in the shared kitchen, too tired and hungover to even think about heading out somewhere, and barely able to pour themselves a bowl of cornflakes, let alone whip up some breakfast. Frederick had come in with a bag from the supermarket, worked some magic with eggs, and produced something unlike anything she'd ever tasted. Not wanting to be outdone, Vannie had made them smoothies with the fruit Frederick had got, and Harry had sloshed leftover vodka into his. Ellie had praised their efforts with every mouthful, while Safet had devoured it all at the speed of light, nodding his approval. God, that seemed so long ago.

'Do you still make those? Ivy adores cooking. She'd love that recipe.'

'I haven't for years,' Frederick said. 'But I'm sure I still could. Maybe once we get out of here, I can have a go.' He paused. 'So Ivy... she likes to cook?'

Jules nodded. 'Yup. She's teaching me, actually.' She let out a breath when she thought about how Ivy was only a few years younger than they all had been when they'd been here. 'How did you feel when you found out you had a daughter?' Jules asked tentatively. She still couldn't believe it. It was so much to take in, now of all places... in the middle of the danger they were facing.

The only sound in the space was the running water.

Then Frederick sighed. 'It was a strange feeling, a mixture of happiness and sadness. I was shocked when I got the match. Shocked, but excited too. But then... then when I got Ivy's email and I learned you were her mother, that changed everything.' He let out a long breath. 'Because of what I thought I'd done to you, and how she was conceived. I couldn't even imagine what you must have gone through. Honestly, I couldn't sleep for weeks.'

He was silent for a minute. 'Over the years, I suppose I'd managed to put all of that to the back of my mind – what Vannie told me, and why I left. I had to, or I wouldn't have been able to have any kind of life. But Ivy's message brought it all back again.'

She could hear the torment in his voice, and her heart ached too.

'And, somehow, instead of making it fuzzy, the time and distance made the pain even sharper. That's when I knew I had to come find you. Find you, and talk to you about Ivy. And maybe... maybe really try to come to terms with that night. With whatever happened.'

'I'm so sorry I can't remember more. But...' Jules turned

towards him in the dark. 'I don't know if this helps, but I can't believe you would do something to me – something to hurt me. Drunk or not, I can't imagine it.' She stared into the blackness as if trying to see into the past.

'It does help.' Frederick's voice cracked. 'It really does. And I'm so relieved you haven't been dealing with the trauma of it for years, like I pictured. That's something, anyway.'

They were silent again for a minute, then Frederick's voice came through the darkness once more. 'And I have to say, I'm impressed with the way Harry stepped up to be with you. Obviously, he believed he was the father, but still... it must have been a shock. I know having a child was always going to be difficult for him.' He paused. 'I hope finding out the truth won't be too painful.'

Jules swung towards him again. 'What do you mean, "having a child was always going to be difficult for him"?' Did Frederick mean because he'd always thought Harry was selfish? She recalled their first few months in student halls, when Harry would constantly eat all the food that was meant to last everyone a week. It had driven Frederick crazy, but when he'd tried to talk to Harry about it, Harry had shrugged and said he could buy more. Jules had stepped in to make sure the fridge was topped up from then on – she had the money, after all – but she'd never forgotten the expression on Frederick's face. He'd stayed friendly to Harry, but Jules could see what he really thought of him... especially when he'd gone out partying, leaving her home alone after her mother's death.

That must be it, but there was something about how he'd said the words that made her think it was more.

'Well, he...' Frederick paused. 'He never told you?'

Jules grimaced. 'Told me *what?*'

'It was the first month we were settling into the halls,' Frederick began slowly. 'Your mum and dad came up and took us all out for a meal, remember?'

Jules nodded, her mind flashing back to that night. She'd been so proud of her beautiful mother and handsome father, and how gracious and charming they'd been to the whole group. Even Safet and Ellie had come out of their shells as they downed cocktail after cocktail, staying until the posh restaurant had kicked them out. Jules had gone to bed that night, flush with happiness and the knowledge that everyone envied her and her family. She'd felt so lucky.

'Harry dragged me to some club afterwards. He was rather drunk, and things got a little... sloppy with some girls. One of them invited him back to theirs.'

Jules let out a breath. That didn't surprise her. They hadn't been officially together then, not until around Christmastime. She knew he'd slept around; that girls were throwing themselves at him. It had made their relationship seem even more special: that he could have had anyone, and he'd wanted her. She could have had anyone, too, but she'd been too busy enjoying flirting with the men around her to commit to anyone. She and Harry had been alike that way.

She rubbed her arms, remembering the moment when they'd first got together. She and Vannie were leaving the next morning to go to her parents' for the holidays, and they'd come back home after a no-holds-barred session at the club. Vannie had fallen asleep, slumped over at the table, and Harry and Jules had crashed out on the sofa. From upstairs, she could hear the soft voices of Ellie and Safet, cloistered in his room, as usual. They'd invited them out, but Ellie had still worn that hurt look because she hadn't been invited along with Vannie to Jules's for Christmas. But surely she couldn't have expected it? She had a family, even though she never talked about them. And she and Jules were nowhere near as close as Vannie and Jules were.

She'd been about to ask Harry to get her another drink when he'd leaned towards her and kissed her. One thing had led to another, and Harry had ended up coming with them to her parents' house. He'd got on like a house on fire with Jules's dad, and Jules had loved watching them together. Vannie hadn't been thrilled to have Harry there, but he'd left to go to his mum's after a few days and she'd perked up again. But Harry hadn't forgotten their night together, like Jules had thought. He'd texted and called, and when they'd returned to Uni, they'd been a couple.

'Well, that's hardly news, that he slept around,' she said to Frederick. 'Anyway, it was so long ago now. It doesn't matter.'

'Yes. I know.' Frederick paused. 'But that's not it. I handed him a condom. You know how they gave out loads at Freshers' Week? He was so out of it I didn't think having one would cross his mind, and the girl, well...' His voice trailed off. 'I thought it would be a good idea.'

'OK.' Jules wondered where this was going.

'And he laughed and said not to worry, that he couldn't knock anyone up – at least without some help from the doctors, or something like that. That he had one of those illnesses as a teen that can affect your fertility.'

Jules stared into the darkness as if it could help her make sense of this.

'I wasn't sure I'd heard him properly, as he was so drunk. So I asked him the next morning. I don't know why – it was none of my business, but I was curious, I guess. He went bright red and told me to fuck off.' Frederick moved, and the crate creaked beneath him. 'I don't know. Maybe I heard him wrong, but I don't think so. He never said anything?'

'No.' Jules could barely get out the word as she tried to process what Frederick had told her. Harry had thought he wouldn't be able to get her pregnant – get anyone pregnant without help? He'd known this, and he hadn't said a word? Hadn't said anything, even when she'd told him she was pregnant with Ivy?

Had he been happy, like Frederick had said, or had he

suspected... she swallowed. Suspected she'd slept with someone else? But surely he couldn't think that. He'd never have proposed if he'd believed she'd been with another man. Got *pregnant* with another man.

And... she wrapped her arms around herself. Maybe he'd learned before he'd proposed that he could get someone pregnant, after all. Because he obviously could, given the twins. And he'd always talked about filling the house with kids. If he'd known otherwise, that would have been plain cruel. True, it hadn't happened, but that was more because they'd been so busy, so tired, than anything else.

God, her head was hurting trying to process everything.

'Are you OK?' Frederick's voice cut into her thoughts. 'I hope I haven't made things worse.'

'No, not at all,' she answered automatically, although it did make her feel more anxious about telling Harry. Because... she breathed in. She *was* going to tell him. Finding out about Vannie and all she'd known – all she'd kept from Jules – had made her see that she didn't want to linger in the dark anymore. She wanted to know the truth, and she wanted Harry to know too. As hard as it would be, he deserved that.

And while Vannie may have hidden things, Jules realised now that she'd hidden things from herself too. Whenever anything had threatened the life she'd built after losing her mother, she'd pushed it away. Finding out about the twins, even now with Frederick and Ivy... her first instinct had been to keep it all under the surface. But there was too much, and she couldn't do it any longer. She didn't *want* to do it any longer. The only way she could fill that empty space inside was to let in the light.

What would happen? What would Harry say? Could they move beyond the surface to face what lay beneath? She didn't know, and the uncertainty made her quake inside.

But she couldn't pretend any longer.

TWENTY-THREE

VANNIE

Vannie plodded from one room to the next on the ground floor, half-heartedly peering under tables and into dingy corners. She didn't really care where Ahmed had gone, to be honest. She needed to think; to come up with a solution. But her brain was refusing to work. She'd always been able to get out of tricky situations in the past. Now, though... What the hell was she going to do? Could she persuade Ivy not to confront Frederick? How much time would that take?

She couldn't let Jules die, of course. But if Jules and Frederick came out now, with Ivy here, then everything would explode. Harry would know what had happened. Jules would know the truth, and she would never forgive her for ripping apart her family. She'd lose her best friend.

She went outside to the pool area, thinking she'd kill time by checking the small buildings around the perimeter, when she spotted Harry crossing the deck.

'Making sure the twins are OK,' he said, pushing back his hair. 'If anything happened to them, I'd never hear the end of it.'

Vannie thought how that pretty much summed him up: he was checking not because he cared about his children, but because he cared about *himself*. She could see he was worried about his wife in the cellar, but part of her wondered if that was because of what Jules represented to him: the wealthy lifestyle he'd craved; a chance to escape from his past. She'd always known how important that was to him, but she'd believed he'd cared for Jules, too, in his own way. As the years had gone on, though, she'd seen less and less of that affection. Last night was the first time she'd seen him put his arm around Jules in ages.

'What are you doing out here?' Harry asked.

'Looking for Ahmed. He has the keys to the cellar.' She met his eyes, wondering why he was staring at her like that. He couldn't know anything, could he?

'Right.' He drew out the word. 'What are you going to do when you find him, Vannie? When you find the keys? Let them out?' Harry narrowed his eyes. 'Aren't you worried what they might be saying in there?'

Vannie held his gaze. 'What do you mean?' She tried to keep breathing. He *couldn't* know anything. She'd kept it all under wraps. Hadn't she?

'You know what I mean,' Harry said. 'You've known all along. You and Jules thought you were being clever, hiding it from me.' His face contorted into a sneer. 'But I knew from the start too.'

'What?' Her chest was heaving, and she could tell Harry was enjoying this.

'I know Ivy isn't my daughter.' The words fell like hammers from Harry's mouth.

'But... but...' Vannie sputtered. 'How?' Had Ivy somehow managed to talk to him in the chaos of the events today? He'd said he'd always known, though, so that couldn't have been it.

'I can't get anyone pregnant,' Harry responded. 'I had mumps when I was a teen, and it affected my fertility.'

What? Vannie's mouth dropped open. 'But what about the twins?'

'Oh, the twins.' He snorted. 'What a shit show. Marta told me to pay up or she'd tell Jules about the affair. I knew they couldn't be mine, but I gave her some money to shut her up. Marta didn't stick to the agreement, though, and ran off to squeal to Jules, anyway. When Jules told me she'd already agreed to pay for them, it was easier to go along with it than to tell her the truth. Things were bad enough as it was.

'Jules never realised I knew, of course,' he continued. 'But when she came to me and said she was pregnant, I knew it couldn't be mine. And I knew whose it must be. The only person it *could* be.' His eyes lasered into her. 'The one person who could ruin everything – all the plans I'd made for my future. All the plans you were supposed to help me with, remember? In exchange for me keeping quiet?' He shook his head. 'Fat lot of help you were. You're lucky he took off.'

Vannie blinked, thinking luck had nothing to do with it. God, how she wished she could change everything; wished she could turn back time to that night, so long ago and yet still so vivid in her mind. Even now, she could remember every detail: how she'd been pouring herself a drink in the kitchen when she'd heard shouting upstairs, and how she'd seen Jules storming down the steps away from Harry.

'That's it,' Jules had fumed as she blew by Vannie, tears streaking down her cheeks. 'I really can't take this anymore.' She'd wiped her face. 'He told me he was tired of hearing about my mum. That I should get over her not leaving me a letter. Get over it!' She grabbed a bottle of something – vodka? – on the counter and started swigging it.

Vannie cursed Harry under her breath. What the hell was he thinking? He really couldn't cope with her sadness, could he? If he wanted to be with Jules, this was hardly the way to keep her – or to keep her away from Frederick. But then he had her for that, didn't he? she thought bitterly.

'Jules, you know what guys are like,' she started. 'They—'

But Jules had spun away from her before she could finish, and a minute later, Vannie heard the splash of the water as Jules dived in the pool. She was about to follow her when her stomach lurched, and she knew beyond a shadow of a doubt that she was going to be sick. She dashed to the nearest toilet, vomiting up the lunch of mussels she'd thought were so delicious. Again and again, as time blurred and the world spun. Cold sweat covered her and she was shaking, unable to move yet knowing she had to. She had to talk to Jules. She had to convince her that Harry was exactly what she needed.

But when she'd dragged herself to her feet and splashed water on her face, what she heard made her go cold and nauseous all over again: Jules's and Frederick's low voices coming from Jules's *bedroom*. Her heart beat fast. Had they kissed? Had sex? If Jules slept with Frederick, that would be it. Jules might love male attention, but the reality was that she'd only had sex with Harry. She was surprisingly traditional that way, saying that her mum had only ever slept with her dad, and she wanted that same kind of committed relationship. Vannie's stomach turned once more as she thought of Jules's mum, and she forced herself to focus.

She couldn't let this happen. She gnawed on her lip, thinking about what to do. As she stood there, the door opened and Frederick came out, wearing only a pair of boxers. She edged forward to see Jules passed out on the bed. She was naked, and Vannie's heart sank. They must have had sex. Jules would wake up, full of love, the star in her very own romance with a man who adored her, like she deserved. She would tell Harry to fuck off like she should have so long ago, and Harry would be furious. He'd be furious, and—

She had to do something. *Anything*. Jules would sleep now until morning, and if she'd drunk as much as she usually did, she might not even remember what had happened. If Vannie could convince Frederick not to say anything, then Jules would never have to know they'd slept together. It would give Vannie more time to think about what to do – how to keep them apart.

'Oh!' She gasped as Frederick came out of the bathroom.

He gave her a funny look when he noticed her hovering outside the door. 'Look, I know you care about Jules,' he said. 'I'll take care of her, I promise. I'll make sure she keeps in touch. You can even come visit!' He smiled then.

Her heart crashed. This was going from bad to worse. What was he talking about?

'Visit where?' she asked, not sure she wanted to know. Her stomach was stirring again, and she could feel the bile building.

'Asia. We've decided to go travelling for the next few months... maybe the next year. I'm sure Jules will fill you in.' He yawned. 'Good night, Vannie.'

'No.' The word burst out of her. 'No, no.'

'She'll be fine.' Frederick took a step towards the door. 'I'd never do anything to hurt her. You know that.'

'That's exactly it, though.' Vannie's mouth went dry as an idea started to form. 'That's what you say. But she told me different.' She paused, wondering if she could really do this to the man in front of her. It would destroy him... but it would also get rid of him. It would get rid of him, and Jules would never need to know what had happened. It was unlikely she'd remember, if she'd been drunk. And on the off chance she did, then this would certainly stop her from tracking him down. She swallowed, forcing herself to continue as the narrative grew and took root in her head.

'What do you mean?' Frederick was looking at her with a confused expression.

'I just talked to her,' Vannie said, praying he wouldn't see that Jules was still out like a light. 'She is in absolute pieces. She says she told you to stop. That she wanted to stop, but you kept on going.'

'What?' Frederick drew back, his eyes full of horror. 'No. That's not true. Let me talk to her.'

But Vannie stepped in front of him, pulling the door closed. 'No. She doesn't want to see you. Please respect her wishes.'

Frederick's stare lasered into her as if he could comprehend better. 'I need to see her. You have to understand. I would never do that to her. I love her. If she wanted me to stop, then I would have listened. I—'

The anguish was dripping from his voice, and for a second, Vannie wanted to stop; to take it all back. But she couldn't. She'd gone too far now, and she couldn't let them stay together. That would ruin everything.

'I can see you've been drinking,' she said, interrupting him. 'I know you're not used to it. You were caught up in the moment, and you've wanted Jules for so long, haven't you?'

Frederick was still staring, but he didn't say a word. He put a hand to his head, like he would collapse if he didn't. Vannie felt a tiny bit of triumph mixed with the guilt. She'd done it now.

'I think it's best if you go,' she said, her voice low and even.

'Go?' Frederick lifted his head. 'It's the middle of the night. And I need to talk to Jules. I can't leave her like this. *Thinking* like this.'

But Vannie stood her ground. 'I can't let you do that. She doesn't want to see you. If you really love her, you'll understand that and you'll go. And if you don't, well...' She blinked. 'I will need to get the police involved.'

Frederick's eyes went wide. 'No, please don't do that. I'll get my things. I'll go now.'

And that had been that. He'd left after packing, disappearing in a taxi. Vannie had eased into the bedroom, grabbing Jules's jogging shorts and a tank top and manoeuvring her into them. Then she'd lurched to the toilet and thrown up again, although whether it was from what she had done or the dodgy mussels, she didn't know.

In the morning when Jules had awoken, Vannie told her Frederick had said nothing happened and that he'd gone. Jules had been heartbroken – too heartbroken to muster up the energy to break up with Harry; too heartbroken to reject Harry's idea of moving in together. Vannie had done what Harry had asked, and he hadn't threatened her anymore. He and Jules moved in together, and Harry seemed to be making a real effort.

Then, one month later, Jules had told her she was pregnant.

'Why didn't you say anything?' Vannie asked Harry twenty years later. 'You said you'd tell her everything if I didn't keep Jules and Frederick apart. Why didn't you?'

Harry shrugged. 'Why would I? Jules was obviously keen to believe the baby was mine, and Frederick was gone. And, actually, you did me a favour. The pregnancy worked to my advantage. It gave me a reason to propose; to up the ante. And what I knew...' He paused. 'What I *know*, well, I didn't want to give that up if I didn't have to. Far better to tuck it away for the future, when I might need it.'

Vannie's pulse raced. Did he mean to use it now?

'Are you going to tell her?' She tried to make her voice strident and strong, but she could hear a tremble in the words.

Harry shrugged once more with a half-smile, and she fought the urge to punch him. 'I could. And the police, of course. Quite sure they'll be interested in hearing all about it. Fleeing the scene... failure to report a suspicious death... lots of scope for investigation there.'

She stared. She couldn't find any words. The police? He couldn't be serious. It had been years ago. And the police didn't investigate suicides, did they? Surely he wouldn't go that far. But even as she thought it, doubt curled inside. Maybe he would.

'But there is something you can do, and I'll keep quiet,' he was saying.

She forced herself to focus. 'What is it?' she asked. Her heart pounded with a mix of fear and dread. What was he going to ask her this time? Whatever it was, she had to do it. She had to, or everything would be ruined.

The seconds felt like forever until Harry smiled. Smiled, and held up... she squinted, then gasped. Was that... was that the key ring? The key ring that had been under the pillow in her room? The key ring with the key to the cellar door?

How had he got it? Had he found Ahmed, and he really did have the keys?

'How did you get those?' she asked, her voice shaking. Did he know that she'd had them earlier, and she hadn't let out his wife and Frederick?

His smile grew wider, reminding her of a predator about to devour its prey. 'While you were chatting with Ivy in your room, Nicola told me you'd magically managed to locate them.' He raised an eyebrow as if he doubted the story. 'It took me all of one minute to find them when I was pretending to look for the first-aid kit.'

Vannie swallowed. She should have hidden them better, but she hadn't been planning to keep them there. Not until Ivy had found out about Frederick.

'I thought you'd be rushing to let her out. But you didn't, and that made me think. Think about what was at stake for you, and how worried you must be. So worried, maybe, that you'd be willing to keep Jules in there, despite the danger. Such a good friend.' He smirked.

Bile rose inside Vannie.

'If Jules and Frederick died, then you wouldn't have to worry any longer, would you? Not about me finding out about what happened that night. Not about Ivy. Your secret would be safe.'

No. Vannie shook her head. She'd let Jules stay in there a bit longer, but she'd never want her to come to serious harm. She'd never want her to die.

'But of course I already knew about Ivy, anyway. I already knew you'd fucked everything up. For *everyone.*'

Panic flooded through her as his words echoed in her mind. *For everyone.* He was right. It wasn't only Harry or Jules or Ivy's lives she'd ruined. It was so much more than that; so much worse than that. And Harry knew... knew everything.

Harry tilted his head. 'Your secrets aren't safe. Well, not unless...'

'What do you want me to do?' The words came out in a croak.

Harry took a step closer, his eyes gleaming. 'I'm going to take a page from your book. I'm not going to open the door. That should suit both of us.'

Her eyes bulged. *What?* He was going to let his wife drown? No. She must not have heard him properly. It couldn't be that.

'There's just one problem. Everyone knows there *are* keys to open the door. And once people realise Ahmed doesn't have them, they're going to start looking somewhere else... at someone else. Keys don't disappear on their own. Someone had to have taken them.' He drew in a breath, looking unblinkingly at her. 'I can't be under any suspicion. I need you to say that you had them.'

She stared, still struggling to take it all in. This wasn't possible. He couldn't mean what he was saying.

'You have a choice,' he continued. 'You can say that you had the keys. You can make up some bullshit like you dropped them in the mud and couldn't find them, or... I don't know. People won't think you have a reason to hurt Jules. You're her best friend, after all.' His face twisted. 'I'll stay quiet about everything else, and you keep your life intact.' He paused. 'Or I tell everything – *and* that you had the keys. You lose it all.'

Anger and disbelief began to build inside as she continued to stare at him. He was going to do this. He was going to let his wife die. No matter what she chose, Jules and Frederick lost their lives. Did he really expect her to let the person she loved most drown? He couldn't, could he?

And why? Why would he do something so brutal? He couldn't be that upset at the truth coming out about Ivy. She knew he was proud, but not enough to let Jules die, surely. It wasn't like he'd just found out either; he'd always known. And while Harry might not love his wife, he did love the life he had with her. If she died, that would stop. He must know that. So what was he doing? Maybe she could convince him to stop all of this. She had to.

'Harry, you do know that if Jules dies, everything will change, right? She's the one who got you that job with her father in the first place. She convinced the board to promote you, time and again.' She paused, remembering Jules saying once that she'd become a one-woman band for Harry to get him the position he'd wanted. And for Harry that power was everything. 'With her father retiring soon, isn't this a critical time for your work? You'll need her influence as much as possible.' Her gut clenched that she had to appeal to his ambition for him to save his wife, but she was desperate. Hopefully, her words would land on something.

But Harry laughed. 'I was going to lose that, anyway. Nothing she could say would make a difference.'

Vannie blinked. He was going to lose his job? 'You'll need her even more, then,' she said. 'You know she has more than enough to support you until you find something else.'

'Even she doesn't have enough to get me out of this,' Harry responded.

'Her father, then.' Vannie was clutching at straws.

Harry laughed again. 'He won't be giving me anything. Not after what I've done.'

Vannie raised her eyebrows. Thomas loved Harry. What the hell had happened?

'This weekend was going to be my chance to talk to Jules,' Harry said. 'See if we could sell the house, buy a smaller flat somewhere. That money would have been a good start.'

Vannie gulped. *A good start?* How much did he need?

'But then bloody Frederick turned up. And Jules started getting all antsy, drinking herself into oblivion like she does when she's nervous. She wouldn't even listen to what I was saying about selling the house, and I needed to at least get her signature on those papers today. That was my last chance.'

Last chance for what? Vannie bit back the question, not wanting to interrupt him.

'And then she and Frederick got trapped in the cellar. At first, I was frantic, of course. I was desperate to get her out and try to convince her to sign. I knew it would be hard, but I could persuade her. She always does what I want. And then...' He let out a breath. 'The cellar started to flood, and we realised that Jules and Frederick could die. I was even more worried. I needed her. I had to get her to sign that paper.

'Then Ivy showed up, and Nicola told me you had the keys. You hadn't let them out, and I started thinking. Thinking maybe you had the right idea: keep them in there. It's best for you – and best for me. Because when Jules dies, who do you think will get everything? The house, the money she got from her mother... it will all go to me.'

Vannie's heart crashed. Oh God. Now, she understood. Now, she understood everything. Horror gripped her as the man in front of her coolly contemplated the possibility of killing his wife as if it was no more than having a sandwich with mayo or not. And she'd given him the idea?

She'd never wanted Jules to die. She couldn't imagine life without her. That was why she'd done so much to make sure things stayed the same.

'But...' She swallowed, desperately trying to think of something. Even if Harry had been with Jules for her money – for her family's money – they had built a life together. He must have some good memories and some affection for her. You couldn't be with a person that long and not have some care for them. And for Ivy and the twins. If Harry wouldn't save Jules for himself, then maybe he would for the children.

'You can't take Jules away from Ivy,' she said, praying she would somehow get through to him. 'Think about what that would do to her.' As soon as the words were out, she realised she'd forgotten Harry knew Ivy wasn't his. Her mind kept working as she tried to think of something else to say to make him change his mind; to get through that cold, ruthless exterior she'd never seen but had always suspected was there. Time was ticking. The water was rising.

'Of course you'll never tell anyone this – not that anyone is going to believe you, anyway,' Harry said. 'And you know what will happen if you do. I'll let everyone in on your secret. And you don't want that, do you?' He raised his eyebrows, and anger and hatred ballooned inside Vannie, pushing away the fear. 'Even if Jules is gone, Ivy will never forgive you. And the police... Your life could still be ruined. Don't forget that.'

Vannie winced. Don't forget that? As if she ever could. As if she ever had. Her whole adult life had been shaped by it: by the fear of what could happen if the truth got out. The threat of what she could lose had made her do terrible things, and the guilt had weighed her down. Nothing in the years gone by – no matter how much she achieved at work or in her personal life – could ever lessen that.

Harry let out a low laugh. 'You and me, Vannie, we're two of a kind. Willing to do anything to get what we want. To *protect* what we have.'

Vannie's head snapped up. That wasn't true... was it? Then

she thought of how much she'd wanted a family, and all she'd done to get it. The lies she'd told and the hurt she'd caused to protect it. Maybe they *were* two of a kind. The thought made her shudder.

But as she held Harry's gaze, a realisation slid in. She wasn't like Harry. Yes, she'd made mistakes. She'd hurt people and destroyed lives. But it wasn't only about her. It was about Jules: the sister and the support she'd never had... and then Ivy. That had been what she was protecting, then and now. The love between them, unlike anything she'd ever had.

She wasn't like Harry at all.

She wasn't going to agree to his plan. She would *never* agree to a scenario where Jules died. There was no time to waste; no time to think; to develop more strategies and lies. Maybe she couldn't protect herself any longer. And maybe she couldn't protect Jules from the secret she'd been hiding, if Harry chose to tell it. But she could save Jules. She could save her life.

She had to get those keys.

Determination mixed with rage overtook her like hot water was rising inside her as floodwater was in the cellar, threatening to claim her too. But this time she didn't want to hold it back. She didn't even try. She wasn't going to let Harry overpower her. Nothing could overpower the love she had.

As if her body was acting of its own accord, she grabbed Harry, raking at his hand to try to grasp the keys. Harry let out a yell and tried to jerk away, but she was holding him tightly. Unsure where the strength was coming from, she continued to try to grip on to him even as he thrashed back and forth.

'Get off me!' Harry yelled, his voice echoing around the pool.

She strained to reach, her heart lifting as her fingers closed around the key ring.

But as she was about to move away, Harry managed to draw

back and shove her so hard she lost her balance. She cried out as she flew backwards. Her head thudded against the hard cement, and the blackness closed in.

TWENTY-FOUR
ELLIE

Ellie searched through room after room, listening as calls rang out through the villa in a bid to find Ahmed. She couldn't believe what was happening. He must be terrified right now. *She* would be terrified, and she hadn't been through half of what he had. She prayed she'd be the first one to track him down, but after looking through every room in the basement, he was still missing. She went back up the stairs to the ground floor, every step feeling like a mountain.

'We can't find him. We're going back to the annex.' Mia appeared, with Nat and Victoria flanking her shoulder.

'Jules will be OK, won't she?' Nat was biting her lip anxiously.

'Of course she will,' Mia said confidently. 'Don't be an idiot. She's not going to *die*.'

Ellie drew in a breath, thinking how the twins had no idea how harsh the real world could be. They'd been wrapped in cotton wool for so long, sheltered from a place where consequences could touch you... where your parents and how much money you had couldn't save you. Bad things did happen.

People did die. And actions did have consequences. She knew that better than anyone.

'It's, well, we weren't very nice to her,' Nat was saying. 'Ever.'

'Why should we be?' Mia responded. 'Mum's always saying she's trying to get Harry to cut us off, and that he's barely giving us any money as it is.'

Ellie raised her eyebrows. Given what she'd seen from the girls' clothes and make-up, she hardly thought that was true.

A sharp shout drifted into the house, and she paused. Was that Harry? Had he found Ahmed? She tried to determine where the noise had come from. Was it outside? She rushed to the pool area, the girls at her heels.

'Oh my God.' She caught her breath at the sight. Vannie was on the ground, her head oozing blood. Was she dead? Ellie couldn't tell, but she was lying so still and her face was so pale that the blood looked even redder.

'I don't know what happened,' Harry was saying. 'I found her lying here. She must have slipped and hit her head.'

Ellie looked down, relief flooding through her as she noticed Vannie's chest moving. She was alive, thank goodness. 'I'll stay here with Vannie and the girls. You go get some towels and blankets to cover her. I don't think we should move her.'

Harry nodded and hurried back into the villa. On the ground, Vannie was groaning. Ellie touched her arm, hoping she would be OK.

Minutes passed, and her desperation to find Ahmed was growing. Where could he have gone? She looked into the fields, hoping to glimpse movement somewhere in the vast expanse, but there was nothing. At least it had stopped raining. Guilt flowed through her that she hadn't supported him. No wonder he'd run.

She heard a faint noise, and she glanced down to see Vannie's lips moving. Ellie leaned closer to listen.

'Harry has keys.'

The words emerged so slowly and so faint that Ellie thought she must have heard Vannie wrong. She leaned closer.

'Please.' The word trickled from Vannie's mouth. 'Get the keys from Harry, before it's too late. You open the door. Hurry.' The last word eked out of her, and she closed her eyes as if it had drained every bit of her energy.

Ellie stared at the woman lying on the ground. Was she delirious? Did she even know what she was saying? Why would Harry, of all people, have the keys? She narrowed her eyes, her mind racing. Maybe he'd found them somewhere. Maybe in all the confusion of finding Vannie, he'd forgotten to tell them. Maybe he was letting Jules and Frederick out right now – perhaps that was why he was taking forever to return.

Finally, Harry came back into the pool area, his arms laden with towels. She craned her neck, but there was no sign of either Jules or Frederick.

'You didn't get them out?' she asked.

Harry blinked. 'What do you mean?'

'Vannie told me you have the keys,' Ellie said.

Harry's eyes bulged. 'She told you I have them?' He met Ellie's gaze, then turned his pockets inside out and held out his empty hands. 'I don't know why she'd say that, but I don't. I wish I did. I wish a million times over that I did.'

'What's happening?' Ivy came into the pool area, her face draining of colour as she looked down at Vannie. 'Oh my God. Is she OK?'

'I think she'll be all right,' Ellie said. 'But she took a big knock on the head.'

'Has anyone found Ahmed yet? Or the keys?' Ivy's eyes were wild.

'I'm afraid not, Ivy.' Ellie gazed across the field towards the wine cellar, scouring the treeline for any sign of her son.

'We have to get them out of there.' Ivy's voice shook. 'Or

stop the water. Or something. We're running out of time.' A tear streaked down her cheek. 'I can't let Mum die in there.' She swiped it away. 'I'm going to go check on her.'

'I'll come with you,' Harry said.

Ellie nodded. Maybe they could have another go at breaking down the door. They had to do something. Ivy was right: they couldn't stand by and let their friends die. They had to get them out.

'Girls, can you please stay here and make sure Vannie is OK? I'm going to go with Harry and Ivy.'

Victoria and the twins nodded with wide eyes, for once struck silent.

Together, the three of them squished across the sodden field, the soggy ground pulling at their feet with every step. They reached the top of the stairs leading into the cellar, and they froze. The steps were swallowed up by water, with only the last three or four at the top in sight.

Ivy gasped and covered her mouth. 'Oh my God.' She swung towards Ellie. 'The water can't have gone up that high inside, could it? There's still space for them to breathe, right?'

Ellie could feel the panic rising off her. She felt the same too.

Harry's face was anxious, and she glanced behind her at the lake of shallow water on the field still flowing down the stairs. With the storm easing, their mobiles should be working again soon and they could call emergency services. But given the state of the stairs, the water inside the cellar must almost be at ceiling height now – if it wasn't already. They couldn't afford to wait.

'Let's try breaking the door down again.' Ivy picked up the old axe. 'I don't think it could let in any more water than what's already inside. Anyway, we don't have a choice.'

But Harry was shaking his head, kneeling to show how the waterlogged steps were beginning to crumble. He broke off a piece of stone and held it up. 'It's too dangerous,' he said. 'The steps could give way, and the walls at the side could cave in. I'm worried the whole thing could collapse. And then...'

They stared at each other for a moment, unable to admit defeat. They couldn't give up. There had to be something more they could do.

'I'm going to try digging a trench again,' Ivy said, shaking with tension. 'I'm not going to let her die in there. I'm not.'

'I'll help you,' Harry said. 'Come on.'

Harry and Ivy started back across the field. Ellie followed, scanning the property once more for Ahmed. Where on earth had he gone? She eyed the woods at the edge of the property, praying he hadn't ventured in there. Then she headed towards the villa, where the twins and Victoria were watching over Vannie.

Hopefully, Vannie was still all right. Later, once all of this was behind them, Ellie would ask what she'd meant. Harry clearly didn't have the keys. Why had she said that he did? And if neither Vannie nor Harry had them, then where on earth were they?

She touched her daughter's back. 'Everything OK here?'

Victoria nodded. 'She's drifting in and out, but I've checked her pulse and it seems fine.'

'Well done. Thank you.' She met Victoria's eyes, proud at how calm and capable she was, despite the chaos of the day. She was strong, more than she knew. Maybe Ellie didn't tell her that enough. Maybe that's why she'd felt compelled to lie, and to try to get Ahmed to leave. 'I'm very proud of you, you know. I hope you can believe that.' She sighed. 'I'm so sorry for everything – for how you've felt. I never meant to make you feel as if you aren't an important part of this family. Like someone could come in and take your place.' With a pang, she realised that was the same way she had felt, all those years ago when the Bosnian woman had turned up at their door. 'They never could.'

She put a hand on her daughter's arm. 'You're the most

special thing in the world to me. I know it sounds super cringey, but you really are my greatest achievement.' She meant that with all her heart.

Victoria held her gaze, then she dropped her head. 'I'm sorry for the things I said.'

'Do you really want him to go?' Ellie asked carefully, not sure she wanted to hear the answer. But she had to. The only way she could help her family come together was to face the truth. She swallowed as it hit her that was exactly what she hadn't done with Safet.

'No,' Victoria said softly. 'I don't think so – not really. I mean, I do wish you and Dad didn't spend so much time with him. I miss how it used to be, when the three of us would go for a picnic or to the beach.' A tear streaked down her cheek, and she swiped it away. 'And... I was scared, I guess.' She glanced up at Ellie. 'Scared you might find out.'

Ellie drew back. 'Find out what?'

'I don't want to tell you. I'm worried you'll be upset.'

Ellie put an arm around her daughter. 'I love you,' she said. 'And whatever you tell me isn't going to change that, OK? Nothing you say can.'

There was a pause, and then Victoria gave a slight nod. 'I've been taking some photos,' she said, staring at the ground again. 'And posting them on...' She bit her lip. 'On social media.'

Ellie froze. 'What kind of photos?' she asked, trying not to show her fear as she thought of the hot-pink bra she'd found in her daughter's room.

Victoria's cheeks flamed red, and Ellie knew instantly her fears were accurate. Oh God.

'I'm not the only one. Lots of girls in my class do it,' she said, a defensive tone creeping into her voice. 'All the girls in my class love them. Guys too.'

Ellie tried to keep her face from showing the horror she felt inside. Were the photos out there in the public domain, for anyone to see? The thought was sickening.

'I know it's not right, but...' Victoria's eyes flashed. 'Finally I wasn't some person no one noticed, hanging around in the back of the class. A person no one remembered. Everyone knows who I am now.' Another tear streaked down her cheek, at odds with her defiant voice.

'Ahmed saw the photos one day, and I told him that if he ever said anything, then I'd get him sent away. I sent him lots of messages telling him that, trying to scare him.' Her voice was a whisper now. 'I'm sorry. I know it was wrong. I... I was so angry. Angry he was here. Angry that you and Dad didn't seem to see me anymore.' She sighed. 'That's why I took the pictures and posted them. To be seen again.'

Ellie stared at her daughter, trying to think of what she could say; of how to respond. She was shocked, horrified and panicked at the thought of what her daughter had done. But she could understand her desire not to be the quiet person in the background who everyone ignored; who everyone passed over. Hadn't she been thinking the same thing when she'd come here? Hadn't she wanted to impress them all? If it had taken her until now to realise that the only people who mattered were those you loved, how could she expect the same from her daughter... especially when those she loved had taken their eyes off the ball?

'We'll have to talk about this much more later,' Ellie said. 'But right now you need to delete any photos on social media, and you need to do it fast. Making and sharing images like that if you're under eighteen is illegal.' Panic flashed through her. Could one of the kids who'd seen them have already gone to their parents? To the school? If so, Victoria could be in a world of trouble.

Victoria went white. 'But they're my pictures. I sent them. I can send my own photos around, can't I?'

'Not of that you can't, no.' Ellie looked into her daughter's frantic eyes. 'Not to mention how they could bring the wrong kind of people into your life. Dangerous people, who might want to harm you. Delete them now, OK?'

'I'm sorry, Mum.' Victoria looked paler than ever as the consequences of what she'd done began to sink in.

'I know.' Ellie embraced her once more. There'd be plenty of words, plenty of discussion later. Right now, what Victoria needed was love. 'And I'm sorry too. I'm so glad you told me about the photos. That took a lot of courage.'

Victoria wiped a tear. 'Can I help you find Ahmed? I want to make sure he's all right. And to tell him I'm sorry too.'

Ellie nodded. 'Of course. Let's do it together.' She reached out and hugged her daughter, feeling her relax against her in a way she hadn't for months. 'I love you.'

'Love you too, Mum.'

Ellie smiled. 'Right. Let's see if we can find this boy.'

Victoria smiled back and nodded. At last, it felt like they'd connected again.

Half an hour later, despite calling Ahmed's name in every room of the vast villa, opening wardrobes and looking under beds, they still hadn't seen any trace of him. Ellie was beginning to wonder if he was even here at all. *Could* he have gone outside? She glanced out the window, her heart sinking as she noticed Ivy and Harry frantically digging a trench, still trying to direct water away from the cellar. The storm was over, yes, but the water was everywhere. If they didn't get out soon... if Ahmed was out there... She winced, unable to think of the pain that could lie in their future. She couldn't let that happen. But what could she do?

'Do you want to check on Dad?' she asked Victoria. 'I'm going to have a look around the grounds.'

Victoria's eyes were wide. 'You don't think Ahmed's out there somewhere, do you?' She swallowed. 'That he left?'

'I hope not.' Ellie's voice was grim.

'I want to come with you,' Victoria said. 'I don't want to give up.'

Ellie smiled at the determination in her daughter's voice, echoing what she'd been thinking. 'Come on, then. Let's go.'

They went back outside to the pool area. Vannie was still lying on the ground with her eyes closed. Her face was pale and the bump on her head was even bigger, although the bleeding seemed to have stopped. The twins were watching over her, the sounds of TikTok videos wafting through the air. At least they'd found something to distract them from the situation, she thought. Never had she been more grateful for TikTok.

Ellie sighed, staring at the vast field stretching in front of her. Ahmed was small, but he was quick. Would he be beyond the horizon now, in the vineyards? Or had he gone the other direction, into the woods? Either way, he would be almost impossible to find if he chose to stay hidden. But she wasn't going to stop. She couldn't, especially not now. He'd done nothing wrong, and she hadn't protected him.

Together, she and Victoria walked slowly across the field, the wet ground sucking at their feet. Above them, the sky was clearing, flashes of blue peeking out from the laden grey. The wind seemed to have died down, too, changing from gales to a slight breeze.

'Mum! Look!' Victoria pointed in the distance.

Ellie squinted. It was a blotch of red, like the shorts Ahmed had been wearing. Her heart leapt. Could that be him? It had to be. But why wasn't he moving?

Heart racing, she and Victoria hurried as quickly as the soggy ground would allow towards the shape, slowly coming into focus as they neared. It was someone – someone crumpled on the ground.

Oh God. It was Ahmed.

'Ahmed!' Ellie bent over him. He was soaking wet, his lips blue, his face paler than she'd ever seen. 'Are you OK? What happened?'

She held her breath as she waited for a response. After what felt like forever, he lifted his head. Fear flashed in his eyes, and Ellie put a hand on his arm.

'You don't need to be afraid. I believe you. I believe you didn't take the keys.'

'I'm really sorry, Ahmed,' Victoria said quickly. 'I shouldn't have made you feel afraid about the photos. Mum knows about them now. And I shouldn't have said those things about you. I do want you living with us. All right?'

Ellie could see how hard those words were for her daughter. Never had she been prouder of Victoria.

Ahmed nodded, a shy smile growing on his face.

Ellie helped him sit up, staring into his dark eyes. 'I owe you an apology too. I'm sorry I didn't stand up for you back there. You shouldn't feel like you have to run away.' She shook her head at the memory of his terror. 'I promise I'll do better in the future.'

'You still want me?' His voice was so soft she could barely make out the words.

Her heart ached. 'Of course I do. I always will. You're a part of this family, no matter what. And when you're family, nothing you say or do can change that. Right?' She glanced at Victoria, remembering what she'd told her daughter.

Victoria nodded.

'Come on, let's get you inside the villa and into a warm bath.' She and Victoria pulled him to his feet, starting to move him in the direction of the house, but he resisted their help.

'No. No, I need to do something. I was going to do it when I fell down. I tripped, and then...' He blinked. 'My head was funny and I couldn't get back up.'

No wonder, Ellie thought. He was ice cold, and he'd barely eaten all day. She tried to move him again, but he held firm. He unfurled his hand, and Ellie stared, unable to take in what she was seeing. A *key*? She met Victoria's eyes, thinking she looked just as surprised. Could that be the key to the cellar door? How had he got it?

'I didn't take the key ring from the bedroom,' Ahmed said, a stricken look on his face. 'I was telling the truth about that. I promise. I don't know where the rest of the keys are. I—'

'I believe you,' Ellie said again, cutting him off. He shouldn't feel like he had to explain. He didn't need to. 'I know you didn't.' He'd tell her when he was ready. She'd trust him this time. And right now, it didn't matter. The most important thing was saving Jules and Frederick. Ellie prayed with all of her might that it wasn't too late. 'However you got this, well done, Ahmed,' she said.

His cheeks coloured, and Ellie squeezed his shoulder. They would talk more later, but right now she had to open the cellar door.

'Victoria, can you take him back to the house and tell your dad what's happening? I'm going to let out Jules and Frederick.'

Victoria nodded, and the children set off slowly back towards the villa. Ellie gripped the key, her heart pounding. Please God, may they still be alive. Please may it not be too late.

Close to the stairs, Harry and Ivy were still digging in the sludgy ground, mud oozing back in as soon as they made a hole.

Ivy turned towards her, her face panicked. 'It's not working! The ground is too wet.'

'It doesn't matter.' Ellie felt a grin growing on her face as she held out her hand. 'I have the key! The key that *will* open the door.'

Harry swung to face her. 'You found the keys?'

'Not the whole key ring, but hopefully, it's the right one,' Ellie said. 'Ahmed had it.'

Harry went still beside her as if he was processing the words. 'What?' he asked, in a voice she hadn't heard before. 'You got this from Ahmed?'

Ellie didn't bother answering. She didn't want to deal with any more questions or suspicion about her boy and, anyway, they didn't have time for this. She stepped carefully down the stairs, her body sinking deeper into the water with each step. It wasn't cold, but it was so clouded she couldn't see her feet. When she reached the last step, the water was almost up to her chest. She plunged her arm into the murky liquid and felt around for the lock, praying she could get the key in before the water rose higher.

She bit her lip. What if they did open the door and more water rushed in, causing Jules and Frederick to drown? What if, in her attempt to save them, she killed them?

She had to take that risk, she told herself. Waiting could kill them too.

She turned the key in the lock and opened the cellar door.

TWENTY-FIVE
JULES

Everything had fallen silent within the dark room. There was nothing left to say. All she wanted was to get out of here. To talk to Vannie and see if she could say what really happened that night. To tell Harry about Ivy and clear the secrets between them. To discover if, after everything, she could finally be happy.

The water was rising as quickly as ever, and they'd resorted to standing on the crates. Even then, it was up to their chests. The space between them and the murky liquid was decreasing more and more with every second, but Jules didn't feel panic. Only sadness that she might never see Ivy again – and pain that she might never have that life without the protective membrane she'd pulled around herself.

But oddly, though, she felt grateful too. She wasn't living an illusion any longer. The plaster of pretence had been ripped off, and even though she was raw and vulnerable, she felt alive. How ironic that in this situation where her life could be over in minutes, she'd felt more alive than she ever had. And even if it might not last long in the midst of all of this, she was going to hang on to that feeling as long as she could.

She raised herself up on her toes as the water got higher. She'd never have imagined the end would be beside Frederick, of all people, in a wine cellar filling with water, at the very place where he'd left her.

'I'm glad you're here.' The words burst out of her before she could stop them, but what the hell? If you couldn't speak with abandon when you were hours from possible death, then when could you? Although so much had changed, being with him was like coming full circle. She knew now why he'd left, and why he'd come back. He'd blown her life apart once more, but this time it hadn't closed doors: it had opened them. It had opened *her*.

The silence stretched between her and Frederick now, but there was no need for words. Under the dank liquid, Frederick gripped her hand. Even though she should be terrified, she felt a peace wash over her.

Her eyes widened as she heard something scratching at the door. 'What was that?'

There was the sound of liquid swirling, then a slab of light stabbed through the darkness, lighting the oily water. She squinted against its brilliance, her heart pounding. The door was open!

'Jules? Jules! Frederick? Are you all right?'

It was Ellie! Jules turned to Frederick, a smile growing on her face as relief and happiness rushed through her. He clutched her hand, a smile lighting his face too.

'We're here!' he called out.

'Oh thank God.' Ellie's tone was heavy with relief. 'Are you both OK? Can you make your way towards the door?'

'We're fine,' Frederick said. 'We can do that.'

'I can't believe we're going to get out of here,' Jules said. 'I wonder how they got the door open. I guess the manager came with the keys, after all. The storm must be over.' But even as she said that, she sensed it was far from true. There was still so much dangerous water to navigate: talking to Vannie and Harry; helping to support Ivy with the truth. It was scary, but she wasn't going to back down from it now.

'Come on, let's go before the water rises even more,' Frederick said. 'You first, and I'll follow.'

Jules nodded, then launched herself off the crate and into the dark water. Her muscles ached after being still for so long, but it felt good to be moving again, even as she banged her knees and shins on various objects as she tried to propel herself towards the door. The water had almost reached the top of it, but there was enough light coming through to see where it was. She glanced back to see Frederick making his way towards her, and she paused until he reached her side.

'Right, here we go,' he said, squeezing her hand.

Jules pushed through the water, using the sides of the door to propel herself out of the cellar and up the stairs. After a few steps, she was on solid ground. She took in a deep breath, pushing her hair back. The sun was bright on her face and, despite the dirt and leaves clinging to her, in a way it felt like she'd been reborn as she lurched up the last few stairs.

'Mum!' Ivy threw her arms around her, and Jules hugged her so tightly she was afraid she'd hurt her.

Frederick stood beside her, and it was as if everything was in slow motion as she watched Ivy and him stare at each other. In the rain, with Ivy's hair slicked back, it was almost like a mirror image: same eyes, same high cheekbones, same smooth large forehead... Jules swallowed, almost unable to believe this was really happening.

Then Ivy winced and she turned away. Jules flinched, thinking it must be so hard to meet the man you hadn't even known about – a man you'd only just found out was your father. A man Vannie had said had assaulted her mother. For the millionth time, Jules wondered why Vannie had told her that. Soon, she would find out.

'Jules.'

Harry's face came into focus, and she blinked. He put his arms around her, gripping her so tightly she could barely breathe.

'I'm so pleased you're OK. I can't...' He pulled back, staring intently at her. 'I can't imagine being without you.'

Jules held his gaze, emotions tumbling through her. Maybe he couldn't imagine, but now, after being trapped with Frederick, *she* could. Or, rather, she could remember when she had imagined a different path: a path she had almost chosen before Frederick had left, piling more grief and heartache onto her already broken heart. The life she'd had with Harry had shielded her when she'd needed it most, like Vannie had shielded her... like the wine had shielded her. She'd been content to carry on, but no more.

'I think we have a lot to talk about,' she said quietly, and he nodded. They would have all the time in the world later, once she'd had a hot shower and managed to speak to Ivy. Helping her daughter deal with what she'd learned was the most important thing now. That, and talking to Vannie. She glanced around. Where was Vannie, anyway?

'How did you get the keys?' she asked. 'Did the manager finally make it out?'

Ellie shook her head. 'No. Ahmed had the key.'

Jules raised her eyebrows. *Ahmed?* She glanced around once more. 'Where's Vannie?'

'She's back in the villa,' Ellie said. 'She slipped on the pool deck and hit her head, but she's going to be all right.'

'I need to talk to her.' Jules pushed back her wet hair, determination filling her. She was tired, hungry and cold, but she felt stronger than ever before.

She swallowed as the group made their way back to the villa.

She had the feeling she was going to need every little bit of that strength.

TWENTY-SIX

VANNIE

Vannie lay with her eyes closed, the music from the girls' videos drifting in and out of her consciousness. She wanted to move, to talk, but every time she tried, the pain in her head overwhelmed her, and she sank back into darkness. How long had she been lying here? She could only remember trying to get the keys from Harry, and him pushing her. She'd fallen over and hit her head, and then she must have blacked out. Panic hit her when she thought of Jules and Frederick, trapped in the cellar with the water rising. Had she really told Ellie that Harry had the keys, or had she been dreaming? Were they still alive? She had to get up. She had to tell someone about Harry.

She lifted her head, but the pain made nausea rise. With a groan, she slumped to the ground again. Mustering all her energy, she tried once more, her stomach heaving as the world swung around her. Somehow she managed to sit up, the twins looking over at her in surprise.

She was about to attempt standing when she heard voices coming towards her. Ivy, for sure. And was that— She listened carefully, praying she was right and that she wasn't hallucinating.

It was Jules! Her heart leapt and relief poured through her. Despite her hammering head, she forced herself to her feet, desperate to see her friend alive and well... desperate to prove she wasn't dreaming.

'Jules!' Everything inside her glowed with happiness as her friend came into the pool area, but then she froze at Jules's expression. She'd never seen her look like that: a mixture of doubt, determination and anger clouded her face. Vannie swallowed, seeing both Ivy and Frederick flanking Jules on either side. And... oh, God. And Harry.

What had he told her? What did she know? And what had Frederick said? She staggered towards her friend, hoping to put her arms around her to show how happy she was she was alive, but Jules moved away.

'How... how did you get out?' Vannie asked, forcing the words through the blinding pain. She turned to Ellie. 'You got the keys? I did try to tell you,' she said quietly. 'It was Harry.' She looked at Jules. 'He had them. He could have let you out, but he wasn't going to.'

Jules stared. 'What do you mean?'

Harry rolled his eyes. 'Vannie, you really did take a knock on the head, didn't you? What the hell are you talking about? Ahmed had the key. There's no point trying to blame someone else.'

She caught the threat in his voice. But he knew now that she'd been willing to reveal everything to save Jules. He had nothing to hold over her any more. And while Jules might be out of the cellar, she was still in the dark in so many ways. She couldn't save Jules's life only to have her go back to a man who could harm her. Somehow, she had to get Jules to believe her.

'I don't know anything about Ahmed and how he got that key. But I do know that Harry has the key ring. He didn't want to open the door,' Vannie said, trying to stay on her feet. 'He was going to keep you in there to get... to get everything. He's desperate for money right now. A lot of it.'

'What?' Jules twisted to look at her husband.

'Don't listen to her,' Harry said, stepping forward. 'You know I wouldn't do something like that. I love you, Jules.' He paused. 'I never would have proposed in the first place, if I didn't. Even if...' He dropped his head. 'Even if I did suspect Ivy might not be mine.'

Vannie watched Jules's face to see her reaction. Had Frederick told her what happened that night? Had he told her Ivy had been in touch? But Jules's face stayed still, and for the first time, Vannie couldn't read what her friend was thinking.

'She's trying to cover her back,' Harry was saying. 'She's been lying to you for ages.' Harry put a hand on Jules's arm. 'I know how much you love her, but she's the one who had the keys all along. She...' He paused. 'She was going to let you drown.'

Jules turned to look at Vannie. '*Did* you have the keys?'

'Yes, but Harry took them. He—'

'Check her pockets.' Harry cut her off. 'I can guarantee she still has them.'

Vannie lifted her head. This was ridiculous. 'Of course I don't,' she said, shoving a hand inside her trousers. 'I...' Her voice trailed off as her fingers grazed the bulging key ring. Oh God. 'Harry put that there,' she said quickly, watching Jules's face crumple. 'I swear. He wanted me to take the blame for everything. He must have done it when I was passed out. I had no idea they were in my pocket.' The words came like bullets from her mouth, but she could see by the way Jules was shaking her head that they hadn't reached their mark.

'Why should I believe you?' Jules asked. 'I know you lied about nothing happening the night I was with Frederick. And probably about what Frederick did too?' She paused, raking her eyes over Vannie's face. 'Because even though we were both drunk, neither one of us remembers what you said happened. I can't believe he would do that. I don't think he did.' Vannie shuddered under her hard stare. 'What I don't understand is *why* you'd say that.' She let out a breath, and Vannie felt guilt sweep over her. 'Were you jealous? Because I was going to be with him?' Jules tilted her head. 'It sounds so petty, but that's all I can think of. Was that it?'

Vannie gazed at the people in front of her. *Jealous.* God, how she wished it was something as insignificant as that. Jules couldn't be further from the truth. She'd loved her. She'd wanted her to be happy. She loved her still, and she knew what she was going to say would end their friendship. It would blow everything apart. And yet it was the only way she could save her – save her from Harry's lies; from his insistence that he hadn't wanted her dead. By coming clean about everything, maybe Jules would believe she was telling the truth about the keys, also. It was a risk, but it was the only chance she had.

And while she may not have had the keys in the end, she *had* locked Jules away for so many years. Locked her away in a place where she couldn't reach the truth. Now... now she really could set Jules free.

Maybe she could set herself free too.

'I never wanted to hurt you,' she began.

Harry snorted.

Vannie flinched, knowing how feeble those words sounded in light of everything – in light of the fact that both Frederick and Jules had almost died. She took a step towards Jules. 'No, really, I didn't. I didn't know... didn't know the horrible chain that would follow.' She paused, conjuring up the words she'd pushed deep down inside. She'd spent so long trying to keep it hidden that it was hard to believe she was going to say what she'd done.

'Do you remember when you and your mum went away to Spain, right after Christmas in our second year at Uni?' Vannie put her hands to her head. She almost didn't want to recall that time, but she had to.

'What does that have to do with anything?' Jules asked.

Vannie willed her to be patient. She had to go slowly here. 'I got locked out of our house, and no one else was around. I knew you had a spare key at your parents', so I went there. Your dad was home.' Even now, she could see Thomas's face clearly in her mind as she opened the door. He'd looked so happy to see her, and Vannie had been missing Jules and Anita so much. Even though she knew the trip to visit Jules's gran at the retirement home was anything but a jolly, she still couldn't help feeling left out.

Jules nodded, and she kept going.

'I asked him for the keys, and he invited me in for a drink. We sat on the sofa and he poured me some of that whisky he likes, and... I won't say I was drunk, because I wasn't. But—'

'No.' The word shot from Jules, who was looking at her in horror. 'No. Dad wouldn't do anything.'

'He kissed me. I kissed him back.' Vannie held her gaze, trying to keep the images out of her mind. How he'd asked over and over if this was OK, and she'd responded by taking off his shirt. How he'd tried to lead her to the bedroom, but she couldn't do that to Anita. How they'd ended up on the floor of the lounge, Vannie squeezing her eyes shut as a photo of Jules stared down at them.

'But you don't even like older men!' Jules sputtered. 'You've told me so many times you'd rather fuck a frog.'

Vannie winced at the words. 'I know. And it's not something I can explain. Your dad, well, maybe it's because I never had a man like him in my life. Caring. Strong. Maybe I was attracted to that.' She paused. 'But it happened. And it kept happening.'

Jules stared. 'What? So you... you and my father, you had an *affair?*'

Her shock and horror was every bit as brutal as Vannie had imagined. She dropped her head, unable to look at her friend any longer.

'Yes. It went on for a year. Not consistently, but on and off.' She'd hated lying to Jules, making up excuses to duck away. She'd hated what she was doing to Anita – betraying her like that, when she'd shown her such love – but she hadn't been able to stop herself. Being with Thomas made her feel safer and more protected than she ever had before. She'd drunk it in, even as she'd known how terrible it was.

She gulped in air, trying to fortify herself. This was where it got really bad.

'Your mother found out. I don't know how, but she did. She confronted your father. I don't know exactly what happened, but she ended up leaving.' Vannie would never forget that awful day Thomas had rung her to say that Anita knew about them, and that she was leaving. Vannie had waited in torture to see if she would tell Jules. A day passed, and then a week, and then...

'Oh my God.' Jules was staring at her as if she'd seen a ghost. 'That was why she left all of a sudden? That was why she wouldn't tell me what had gone wrong?' She paused. 'Do you know how many years I've wondered how it's possible for everything to be so perfect, and then suddenly not? How my vision of their marriage and their love that I'd always hung on to was shattered, and I never knew why?' She shook her head. 'Do you know how angry I was with my mum for not telling me? For leaving? I thought it was her fault. Until she died, I never forgave her. And now I find out it was *you*. You were the reason. You were the reason, and she was trying to protect me. How could you have done this?'

She stepped closer to Vannie, and Vannie could almost feel her rage.

'You ruined her marriage, her life.' Tears streaked down her face. 'Maybe you didn't kill her outright, but you may as well have.'

Vannie tried to stay strong in the face of Jules's words. 'I need...' She swallowed. 'I need to tell you more.' As awful as what she'd said was, it wasn't the worst. Not by far. 'The day your mother died.' Her head was pounding and she swayed, but she had to get it out. 'You called me, remember? Asked me to check on her when you couldn't get in touch?' The memory filtered into her head. No matter how much she had tried to block it out, it was always there, like a nightmare.

'I got to the room before you. I knocked, but she didn't answer, so I grabbed a maid and told her I was locked out. She opened the door, and your mum... She was in the bath. She...'

Vannie paused, remembering the moment she'd discovered Anita in the crimson water. She'd stared for a second, not sure if what she was seeing was real. Not sure if it was actually happening. She'd covered her mouth to muffle the cry and slammed the bathroom door as if by shutting out the scene she could banish it from her mind. She'd stood there for a second, shaking, the guilt and panic making it impossible to process anything.

'I froze,' Vannie said, watching as an incredulous expression came over Jules's face. 'I didn't know what to do. Then I heard your voice. You were on the phone, coming down the corridor, talking to someone. I sneaked outside and around the corner. You never saw me.'

Jules was still staring at her with that expression, and silence swirled around them all.

'You knew my mother was in the bathtub. And you didn't call 999. She could have still been alive! Did you even check?'

Vannie cringed. Jules was right. She hadn't checked, and she'd been too stunned to call 999. And then she'd heard Jules coming, and she'd left. The torment had followed her for years, voices questioning whether she'd wanted Anita to die so the secret could stay hidden. Could she have saved her and chosen not to? It followed her still, and she had no answers. She never would.

'You didn't stop me,' Jules continued. 'You knew I was about to discover my mum lying there like that. And you didn't even try to stop me.' A tear streaked down her cheek, but she didn't wipe it away. 'When I think of my mother now, that's what I remember. Her body in that bathtub. Everything else has been tainted with that. Everything.'

She paused, and silence fell once more. 'And what does any of this have to do with the lies you told about Frederick?'

Vannie swallowed. 'Harry found out about what happened with your dad.'

Jules jerked. '*What?*' She glanced at Harry, who was rolling his eyes.

'Don't believe it, Jules. She'd say anything now.'

But Jules didn't even look as if she'd heard him. 'How did he find out?'

'It was the last week of term, before we moved out of the house. We were packing up our things, about to head off on our trip here after the final few exams. Your dad came to pick up some of your boxes, remember?' Vannie closed her eyes for a second, trying to alleviate the pounding in her head. 'He wasn't... he wasn't in a good way. I think he'd been drinking. And he tried to kiss me.' She couldn't bear to look at Jules to see her reaction. 'Your mum's death tore him apart. He didn't want *me*. He just wanted someone.' She shifted, the pain ripping through her. 'Anyway, I pushed him away, and he got quite upset, talking about what had happened between us and how he felt to blame. Harry overheard everything, and he came to speak to me later that night.' She could still feel her horror when she'd returned from the library to see Harry sitting on her bed, waiting for her.

'He said that he'd tell you everything if I didn't help him.

He said he might even call the police; tell them I'd done some-thing to your mum, since he'd heard me saying I'd been in the hotel that day. I was terrified.' Vannie had felt the ground shaking beneath her. She couldn't bear losing what she'd always wanted. She couldn't bear losing Jules.

She put a hand to her head, hoping it would ease the pain a bit, but it throbbed even more. 'So I told Harry I would do anything. And he said...' Vannie dropped her eyes. 'He said he'd stay quiet, as long as I kept you away from Frederick.' She tried to keep breathing. 'That weekend, he was going to ask you to move in with him. He wanted to be sure you'd say yes.'

'She's lying,' Harry said quickly. 'You know she's lying.'

'Be quiet, Harry.' Jules's voice was colder than Vannie had ever heard it.

'It seemed like such a small thing to do. I mean, I didn't think you and Harry weren't really going to go the distance, anyway. I thought once you moved in together you'd soon see how incompatible you both were. Harry would crash out of the job your dad had got him, and that would be that. But...' She shook her head, the pain almost knocking her out with its force. 'It didn't exactly turn out that way.'

Jules let out an incredulous laugh. 'To say the least.'

'I know. I never meant all of this... *any* of this to happen,' Vannie said. 'But that morning when you woke up after being with Frederick, well... I knew if you two got together, Harry would tell you everything. Our friendship would be over.' She breathed in. 'I had to get rid of him, so I told him that story about him assaulting you. You were so out of it I knew you wouldn't remember anything in the morning. If I told you that you *had* slept with Frederick, you'd probably tell Harry. You wouldn't be able to keep it from him.' She paused. 'So I told you nothing happened. And then when you found out you were pregnant, of course I couldn't tell you the truth. I'd already lied. And if you thought it might be Frederick's, you might tell Harry and it would all fall apart.' She sighed again. 'I had to keep it going.'

'No, you didn't.' Jules's eyes were hard. 'You made the choice to keep it going. Yes, I would have been upset if you'd told me what you'd done. More than upset: devastated. You destroyed my family. You as good as destroyed my mother. We wouldn't have been friends any longer. But this... You ruined Frederick's life.'

Sadness crossed Jules's face, and the guilt clenched Vannie so strongly that for a minute, she felt her legs sag beneath her.

'Things could have been so different.'

Jules turned towards Frederick, and for a second, Vannie could almost see the alternate reality, where Jules and Frederick had a happy marriage with Ivy growing up in their house.

'You took knowing her real father away from Ivy,' Jules was continuing. 'You chose yourself over me. If you'd been a true friend, you would have realised what you should have done.'

Vannie dropped her head. Jules was right. Until now, none of what she'd done had been for her – or for Ivy, despite what she'd told herself. It had been for her. She'd been so desperate for love that she'd let it warp her into harming the very people who gave her that love.

'But I still don't understand why you wanted me and Frederick to drown,' Jules said. 'You couldn't have been sure what Frederick told me in there. And I still wouldn't have known about you and my father... or my mother. It doesn't make sense.'

Vannie nodded, a tiny bit of hope leaping inside. 'I know. It doesn't, because I wouldn't have let you die.' She took a step closer, praying Jules would believe her. 'I wanted to let you out. I was telling the truth. Harry had the keys. He said he'd stay quiet if I said that I had them... that I could make up a story about how I'd misplaced them, then found them too late – anything to deflect the blame from him. He told me that I might lose you, but at least I would still have Ivy. When I tried to grab the key ring from him, he pushed me over.'

Harry rolled his eyes. 'As if *anyone* would believe a word you're saying now.'

Jules stared at her, then back at Harry. Once again, Vannie had no idea what her friend was thinking, but she had nothing left to hide. She'd given all she could to Jules, and now she was empty. She only prayed that Jules would believe her.

Her legs gave out and she sank onto the cold, wet stones.

TWENTY-SEVEN
JULES

Jules watched her best friend collapse to the ground as if revealing the past had drained the life from her. She put a hand to her head, trying to process Vannie's words. Her mother had left because she'd discovered Vannie had an affair with her father. Vannie had found her in the bath that day, and she hadn't done anything to help.

She'd wanted to know the truth. But this... this was more than she ever could have imagined. Despite everything she'd learned, though, she was still standing. Maybe she was stronger than she'd believed. No, she *was* stronger than she'd believed.

'What Vannie's saying is complete bullshit, trying to pin the blame on me.' Harry stepped closer to her. 'I love you, Jules. Yes, I wanted to be a part of your life, but not because of the money. Because of *you*. And I don't care who Ivy's biological father is. I've never cared. She's still my daughter.' He lowered his head. 'When I was younger, I had mumps. Doctors told me I wouldn't be able to get anyone pregnant. Not naturally, anyway.' He looked up. 'Maybe I should have told you, but when you came to me with the news, I wanted to think the doctors had been wrong.'

Jules let out her breath. She was glad Harry was telling the truth now, without her having to ask. That was a start, anyway. And the doctors *had* been wrong, because even if Ivy wasn't his, he'd managed to get Marta pregnant with the twins.

'I haven't been perfect,' Harry was saying. 'I've screwed up a lot. But we have had a good life together, right? Why would I want you dead? You can't seriously believe I would do that to you. Or to Ivy.'

Jules stared at him. It *was* hard to believe he'd want her dead. But then, she couldn't believe Vannie would either. For Harry to let her and Frederick die in such an awful way when he had the key in his hand the whole time, well... there had to be a reason someone would even contemplate such a horrific thing. She closed her eyes. What had Vannie been saying about money? She drew in a breath, remembering how Harry had asked for her signature to sell the house, and how she hadn't wanted to. She would have given it to him if he'd really been desperate, though. He didn't have to let her drown. He could have simply talked to her.

But when had they ever really talked? She gazed at her husband, for an instant seeing the young man he used to be. Sadness shot through her as she thought of the past twenty years. They'd been together physically – most of the time, anyway. But how much had they shared? They'd both been more apt to shove things down, out of the way. That was hardly the hallmark of a good relationship.

She jerked as the realisation hit that they'd *never* had a good relationship... a real relationship. She loved him, but she'd never been in love with him, not like she should have been. It had been the thought of a perfect life that she'd loved. If Vannie was right, Harry had never loved her either. Like her, he'd only wanted that perfect life. That's why they'd pushed down any mistakes and any misgivings. That's why Harry had proposed, and why she'd stayed.

That's why she felt so empty.

And if what Vannie said was true, there was so much more... so much more darkness Harry had kept inside. Could he have threatened Vannie, simply to ensure he'd stay with Jules? Could he be so unfeeling that he'd tried – she swallowed – tried to kill her?

'Jules, let's go.' He took her arm and propelled her inside the house. 'Let's get out of here. Let's go back home, and we can talk about everything away from this craziness.'

She kept staring, her mind spinning. *Had* he done those terrible things Vannie had said? Nausea roiled inside, and she squinted at her husband as if she could see beneath the surface. She couldn't, though. She had no idea what he was thinking; what he was feeling. Had she ever?

'Don't go.'

A voice rang out behind them, and they turned to see Ahmed standing there. He was shivering and his lips were pale, but his back was straight. He was staring Jules in the eyes – for the first time since they'd got there, without the phone as a shield.

'I saw him push her,' Ahmed said. 'She was trying to get the keys from him, and he knocked her over. I saw it. I was leaving the villa when they came out, and I hid behind the pool pump. I saw everything. Don't go with him. Please.'

Jules's eyes widened, and she swung towards Harry. His face was red, and his mouth was opening and closing as if he was gasping to get words out amidst the anger marring his features.

'So Vannie was telling the truth? You wanted...' She paused, trying to muster up the strength to finish the sentence. 'You wanted me to drown?'

'Don't be ridiculous,' Harry sputtered. 'You're going to listen to this little worm? He can barely even speak English.' He turned to Ahmed. 'Stop lying,' he said. 'You didn't see that.'

Ahmed stood firm. 'I'm not lying. I have it on my phone. Here, let me show you. I—'

Before he could get the mobile out, Harry lunged forward and grabbed Ahmed's arm. Ahmed yelped in surprise as Harry tried to take the phone from him.

'Let go of him.' Ellie's face was fierce as she stepped between Harry and Ahmed, forcing Harry to move away. 'I swear, if you touch him again, I'll call the police.' She put an arm around Ahmed, drawing him close to her. 'In fact, I've a good mind to call the police right now.'

'No need,' Harry said. 'We're leaving, anyway. Come on.' He took Jules's arm once more.

She jerked away from his grip. 'No.' She met his eyes. 'I'm not going with you.' She had seen what lay beneath the surface now, and she didn't want to be anywhere near this man. Watching him with Ahmed – seeing that anger unmasked – had shown her that he could be capable of wanting her dead. She didn't need to see the mobile footage to prove that. And at this moment, all she wanted was to think of the future... to *live*. Her mum may not have been able to escape the dark she'd been plunged into, but Jules could.

She turned to Harry. 'You need to go. I'm staying here.'

'I'm not leaving without you.' Harry's voice was low.

He moved towards her once more, but she didn't flinch. She wasn't afraid any longer.

'Yes, you are.' Frederick's voice was strong and certain, and she turned to see him beside her. She touched his arm to show she was fine. 'You are, or I *will* call the police.'

Harry snorted as he stared at them. Then he turned and went upstairs. They heard him moving around in the room before he came back down and slammed out the door. The car engine started, they heard the sound of gravel crunching, and then it was quiet again.

'Thank you,' Jules said softly to Frederick. She turned to Ahmed. 'And thank you too. That was very brave.'

Ahmed nodded and held her gaze for a moment as if he wanted to say something, then turned to look out the window. A beam of sunlight sliced through the clouds onto the watery land. The light was so bright it almost hurt her eyes, and despite everything, calm filtered into her.

The storm was over.

TWENTY-EIGHT
ELLIE

Ellie stood beside Jules and Frederick, the sun turning the room golden. She'd never been prouder of Ahmed. Thanks to him having the courage to speak up, the nightmare had come to an end for Jules. But for her... She breathed in. She needed to talk to Jules to find out what she knew and what she'd told Safet. She needed to try to keep the secret under wraps; to try to save her marriage.

But... she swallowed, thoughts swarming through her mind. She'd seen the damage keeping secrets could cause, especially in a marriage. Jules and Frederick had almost died because of it, and even though they hadn't, their whole lives had been lived under a pretence. Ellie thought of that moment when she'd turned the woman away, worried Safet would leave her to go back home. Would her life have been different if she'd told him the truth then too? Would he have left? She'd endured that fear and uncertainty for so long that it had twisted and turned itself into the fabric of their lives.

She'd seen on this trip that nothing mattered more than her family. She'd been strong enough to stand up for her son –

finally. Could she find the strength now to tell her husband what she'd done so long ago?

'Ellie.'

Ahmed's voice tore her from her thoughts, and she glanced down at him. Despite the incident with Harry, his cheeks had more colour, and something about him seemed more solid; more certain.

'Feeling better?' She smiled down at him, so thankful he wasn't suffering any more serious harm from his exposure to the wind and rain.

Ahmed nodded. 'Yes. But I need to talk to you. Please.'

'OK.' It would be good to give Jules and Frederick some time to relax, anyway, after their ordeal. 'Come, let's go into the bedroom. We can chat there.' She touched her son's back lightly as she steered him down the corridor and onto the soft bed, wondering what he seemed so determined to say to her. Did he really believe they wanted him? After all they had been through, did he want *them*? Fear filtered in as she met his dark eyes. That couldn't be it, could it? Could she have fought for him, only to lose him? Determination replaced the fear. She wasn't going to let that happen. 'What did you want to say? You know I'm super proud of you, right? That took a lot of guts to stand up to Harry.'

'Thanks.' Ahmed squirmed on the bed. 'But...' Silence curled through the room, and then he swallowed. 'I had the key.'

Ellie smiled. 'I know, sweetie. That's how we got Jules and Frederick out. Did you manage to get it from Harry somehow? After he pushed Vannie?'

'No.' He frowned, his forehead creasing. 'You don't understand. I had the key all along.'

Ellie drew back. 'All along? What do you mean?' She tried to stay as still as she could despite her surprise. She could see how hard it was for Ahmed to open up, and she wanted him to keep talking.

Ahmed took in a big shuddery breath. 'The door didn't close because of the wind. I'm the one who closed it.'

What? Ellie tried hard to keep her face calm. 'But... why?'

Ahmed squeezed his hands so tightly she could see his knuckles turning white. 'I was scared. Scared of *her*.'

Ellie blinked. 'Of Jules?'

Ahmed nodded. 'I didn't want to lose my family. Not again.' He jammed his fists into his eyes, and Ellie could see how hard he'd found it to even express such a thought. She wanted to tell him he wouldn't – that he never would – but after what he'd been through, she knew he'd find it hard to believe. 'And I saw Jules's messages on Safet's phone. At home, and then again at supper that first night. I got worried. Why was she texting him so much? Was she going to take him away? She's so pretty. Like the women my brothers used to have up on their walls.'

Ellie smiled at the homely vision of teenagers with posters tacked up in their room. It seemed so normal, despite the constant threat Ahmed had lived with. It was good to hear him talk about his life back in Syria. He so rarely did.

'I heard her tell you that she and Safet needed to talk to you about something, and I didn't want that to happen. I didn't want her to come in and ruin our family.' His face tightened. 'I wasn't thinking. I just wanted her gone, so I slammed the cellar door.'

Ellie nodded, thinking how his fears had mirrored hers. She could understand completely. Sometimes, it seemed easier to shut everything away.

'I didn't know the door would get stuck, but I was glad it did.' He lifted his chin. 'After I closed it, I took the key ring from the hook, where the manager told you it would be. Then I got the key off the ring and put it into my pocket. I put the rest of the keys back on the hook.'

Wow. He must have really been scared to do all of that,

Ellie thought. But then, hadn't she done as much to make sure Safet would never find out about his cousin? Hadn't she been worried about losing him, as well?

'I know it was bad,' Ahmed was saying. 'I know it was wrong, but I wouldn't have let them die. If the locksmith never came, or Ivy couldn't find a way to rescue them, I'd have opened the door. I was going to let them out before I ran away, but then I saw Harry and Vannie, and I hid. I was scared, I tried to run, and...' A tear escaped from his eye, and he swiped at it.

'But why were you running away?' Ellie asked gently, putting a hand on his leg. If he wanted to save his family, it made no sense that he'd leave.

'I couldn't tell you what I'd done,' he said in a small voice. 'The flood, Safet getting hurt... too many bad things had happened because of what I did, even if I never wanted them to. I wanted to tell you when the water kept rising, but then Safet got hurt, and I was even more scared. I thought you wouldn't want me, but I couldn't let them drown. The only thing I could do was to let them out and then go.' Another tear escaped. 'But I didn't want to leave. I really didn't.' He stepped forward, and before Ellie could make a move, he was in her arms.

She drew him even closer as his body shook and sobs tore through him, and it struck her that, for the first time, he felt free enough to let himself go with her. Finally, he trusted her... believed in her.

'I'm sorry,' he said, meeting her eyes. 'I'm so sorry.'

Ellie wiped away her own tears. 'I know you are. And I'm so glad you told me the truth. It means you believe that you really are a member of this family, no matter what.'

Ahmed nodded. 'Can I go find Victoria now? She promised to teach me a dance that everyone does at school.' A shy smile crossed his face. 'I can't dance. I told her that, but she said she'll show me. My sisters used to try to teach me, as well.' He paused. 'My other sisters.'

Happiness swept through Ellie at the thought of her two kids starting to come together. 'Of course. Go.'

He gave her another quick hug, then dashed off to find Victoria. Jules's voice drifted into the room, and Ellie got to her feet. She could go talk to her now. She could find out what she knew and convince her to keep quiet. But... she thought of Ahmed, and how brave he'd been to tell her what he'd done. How he'd trusted her words; her love. And Victoria, too, telling her about the photos and how she really felt. If her children could have such courage, then shouldn't she?

Like her kids, she'd made a mistake – a terrible one. And like them, she didn't want to keep that a secret any longer. She had to trust that Safet would see how sorry she was for what she'd done, and that their love was enough to carry them through. She had to trust that *she* was enough.

She went down the stairs and through to the lounge, then sat beside her husband.

'Victoria has been filling me in on what happened,' Safet said, turning to her with a concerned expression. 'Are you OK?'

'I am.' Surprisingly, she was.

Safet didn't even know the half of it, she thought, still trying to get her head around what had happened to Jules's mum, what Harry had done and the fact that Ahmed had the right key all along. She'd fill him in on everything later. She couldn't keep this secret any longer.

Safet lifted his head. 'Harry's gone?'

'Yes. The storm has stopped. Once the mobiles are working, I'll call and get a medic to come have a look at you. And Vannie too.' She glanced out the window, where it was more blue sky than grey now. The storm had cleared almost as quickly as it had come. 'If the road is passable, it shouldn't take too long for them to get here. I don't know how we've done all of this without you.'

Safet put a hand on her arm. 'You've been brilliant. You don't give yourself nearly enough credit.'

She swallowed. 'Safet, we need to talk.'

He met her gaze. 'I know. We will. But why don't you relax first, get warmed up.'

She shook her head. It would be so easy to put it off, but she didn't want to. 'No, that's all right.' She swivelled to face him. 'Look, there's something I never told you. Something I should have. I've been holding onto it for years, and I can't anymore.'

Safet raised his eyebrows. 'What is it?'

She took in a deep breath. 'A long time ago, when we first moved to London, a woman came to see you – a family friend who was visiting relatives. You weren't home, but I invited her in and she told me that you had a cousin, Amir, who was still living back in Bosnia. He was in a special hospital and needed a lot of care. She gave me the name of the hospital for you to find him.' She met his eyes, which were staring at her incredulously. She knew this would be hard, but it was almost impossible to get the words out. Still, she had to.

'I...' She paused. 'I was afraid to tell you. Afraid you would leave London, leave me and the life we had planned together, and go back to Bosnia.' She shifted on the sofa. 'And so I... I didn't say anything.' She dropped her head. 'But then, before we were about to get married, I decided I would call the hospital and see how he was... put you in touch. I didn't want to keep it from you anymore.'

Safet was still staring.

'And they told me that Amir had died.' Pain stabbed inside her like it was yesterday, and she looked down. 'I couldn't believe it. I'd taken away your one chance to find another member of your family. I was so scared, so upset.'

She dared to look at him, but he was silent.

'I can never say sorry enough,' she said. 'Nothing can

change what I did, but I hope that somehow, you can forgive me.'

The silence stretched between them, and finally he blinked.

'I can't believe you didn't tell me,' he said softly.

Guilt pierced her gut like sharp thorns.

'You knew how alone I felt, and how much I wanted a connection with someone back home. You were the only one who knew that.'

'I know,' she said, holding his gaze.

'And you didn't have faith enough in me – in us – to say what you'd found. You let your fear keep me from my family.'

She could see the pain on his face – pain she had caused.

'I've regretted not telling you every day,' she said, her voice shaking. 'That's not an exaggeration, honestly. If I could go back and fix it, I would.' She put a hand on his arm, praying he wouldn't shrug her off. 'I'm not making excuses for what I did, but if Amir hadn't died, then I would have told you. By the time I called, though, it was too late. He was gone. And how could I say anything then?' A tear dripped down her cheek. *Could* he ever forgive her?

'I wish you had told me,' Safet said. 'Because I would have been able to call myself.' He paused. 'I would have been able to find out that Amir wasn't dead, after all.'

'What?' The words jolted through her. 'What do you mean? When I called, they told me very clearly that Amir Kovic was dead.'

Safet raised his eyebrows. 'My cousin's surname isn't Kovic,' he said.

Ellie sagged back in disbelief. She hadn't even thought about it; she'd simply assumed his surname was the same as Safet's. Oh God.

'He didn't die. He's in Bosnia, and he has a family.'

Ellie stared, unable to respond.

'That's why I was messaging Jules – why she was messaging

me. She's going to start working at the charity, helping refugees trace their families. She decided to start with me. And she found him.' He raised himself up. 'He's alive, and he has a family of his own now. She's been busy seeing if he knows anything about other family members who could still be alive. I wanted to be one hundred per cent sure before I told you. I knew how excited you'd be.' He drew back. 'I thought you would be, anyway.'

Ellie lowered her head. She deserved that. Of course he would doubt her now, like she'd doubted him.

'And, Ellie, if you had told me, I never would have left you. It was never you and my life here, or my family back home.' He gazed steadily at her. '*You* are my home. You and the kids. Not a place, not a country. You gave me that love and comfort. I don't know what I would have done without you, to be honest. You gave me all that I lost. But...' He paused, and her heart dropped. 'I could have spent the last twenty years, knowing my family wasn't completely gone. I could have got to know my cousin better; taken our family there to meet his. I could have known that the war didn't destroy everything.' He blinked. 'It's hard for me to think that the person I relied on to give me the love I was missing took away the chance for me to have all of that.'

'I'm so, so sorry,' Ellie whispered. There was nothing more she could say. 'And of course I'm happy he's alive. I'm thrilled for you... and for us.' She hoped there was still an 'us'.

'I want him to come to the UK,' Safet said. 'Him and his family. They'll need to stay with us until they get settled. It's going to be a little crazy for a while.' He paused. 'But maybe being so busy is a good thing. Maybe we both need some time and space from each other. To absorb what's happened, and—'

'No!' Ellie yelped. 'I don't need time and space. That's the last thing I want.' She gulped, trying to quell the panic. 'I under-stand if you do, though, and of course I'll give you that if you need it.' She would give him anything now, and pray he'd come back to her. He *would* come back to her. She had to trust in them.

'I know how hard this must have been to tell me,' he said. 'And I am glad you finally did. Let's see how things go when we get home, OK?' He touched her arm lightly. 'But no matter what, we will get through this. I believe that. You have to too.' He reached out and wiped away her tears.

She nodded. 'I do.'

The words felt like a vow, one that, for the first time, she could truly commit to.

TWENTY-NINE
VANNIE

Vannie took a final glimpse of the villa as the paramedics helped her into the ambulance. The creamy stones glowed in the sun, the droplets of rain clinging to the ivy shining like jewels. It looked idyllic, every bit as peaceful as that morning after Frederick had left.

She closed her eyes, her head pounding as she remembered how she'd stood in almost this same spot back then, staring at the building as guilt and fear tunnelled through her. She'd prayed then that neither Jules, Harry nor Frederick would find out what had really happened. She hadn't even thought of the possibility of Jules getting pregnant, and how once Ivy had been born, her love for her god-daughter would make that fear grow even bigger.

It was funny, she thought now. All she'd ever wanted was someone to love her for *her*, unconditionally. Her mother had pushed her away. She'd latched onto Jules, desperate to fill that empty space, and then Jules's father... and then done what she could to protect her secrets, fearing all would be ruined if they were uncovered. And she'd been right to be afraid. Jules never wanted to see her again.

Pain shot through her as she thought of her friend and how she'd built her life around her. She'd made mistakes, that much was for sure. She'd told herself it was to protect Jules, but instead it was to protect herself. In the end, though, she had told Jules the truth. She should have years ago. Maybe then this horrific chain of events could have been avoided. Maybe then Jules would have forgiven her – eventually. But she wouldn't regret saying all that she had. She'd owed her friend that much and more.

Perhaps that was unconditional love: giving someone else what they needed and deserved, despite how it would rip your life apart. That's what she'd done now. She *did* know what unconditional love felt like, even if she'd never received it herself.

The paramedic started the engine, and she winced at the sound ricocheting through her head. Soon, all of this would be behind her. She would be back in London, on her own. Nicola had left earlier, staying true to her word not to talk to Vannie again. She wouldn't have expected anything less.

'Vannie!'

Vannie's eyes flew open at Ivy's voice, and she swallowed. Had she come to tell her how upset she was? How let down she felt, and how betrayed? Guilt swelled inside once more as she thought of how she'd told Ivy she'd been the product of an assault. Oh God. How could she have done that to the person she loved so much?

'Ivy, I'm so sorry,' Vannie said, turning towards her god-daughter. 'I lied to you, and I lied to your mother.' She blinked away the tears that had suddenly appeared. She'd been so good at holding it all back until now. 'But you know the truth, and I hope you can get to know Frederick. I hope... I hope you have a good life.'

'How could you tell me that about Frederick and Mum,

Vannie?' Vannie could hear the pain in Ivy's voice. 'How could you let me go on thinking I wasn't wanted?'

Vannie winced. There was no excuse. There was nothing she could say. Her heart ached as she watched the tears streak down Ivy's face.

'And all you were saying about how Mum's mum died...' Ivy wiped her cheeks. 'You were always the one I could talk to. You've always been there for me. I trusted you, and you lied to me.'

'I know.' Vannie's voice was a whisper.

'How can I ever trust you again after this?' More tears formed in her eyes. 'What am I going to do without you?'

'I'm still here. I'll always be here for you.' Vannie reached out and touched Ivy's face, thinking once more how she loved her like a daughter. 'I love you.' She realised with a shock that she'd never actually said those words aloud – to anyone. And despite the mistakes she had made, she did love Ivy with all of her heart.

'I love you too,' Ivy said. 'I'm so, so angry at you, though. Angry, and hurt. Beyond hurt.'

Vannie blinked in surprise. Ivy still loved her. She could still say those words. *This* was unconditional love. Maybe she did have it in return. Maybe in telling the truth, she hadn't lost everything, after all.

'I don't know what will happen in the future. I need time to think about all this. To see if maybe I can trust you again.'

'Take all the time you need,' Vannie said. 'I'll be waiting.'

Ivy nodded, and the paramedic slammed the door. Then Vannie closed her eyes and listened to the crunch of the gravel as the ambulance drove away from the villa.

THIRTY

JULES

Jules opened her eyes the next morning, squinting as the sun flooded through the slanted shutters. The warmth filtered into her, and despite everything that had happened yesterday and all she'd uncovered, happiness filled her as she glanced at the man beside her. She and Frederick had talked for hours last night before falling asleep. This time, with no drink involved, she could remember exactly what had happened. And while they may not have done any more than sleeping side by side, right now that felt exactly right. There was no rush; no hurry. They had all the time in the world.

'Promise me something,' Frederick had said, his voice as warm as the blanket she was wrapped in.

She'd shivered, not from the cold, but from the emotion stirring inside. It had been a long time since she'd felt such desire. She'd almost forgotten what it was like.

'What?' Jules had leaned towards him.

'When we leave this place tomorrow, it's not going to be easy. There's a lot to unravel; a lot to figure out.' Frederick paused. 'Promise me that we won't lose each other again in all of that... in all the complications and the details. I lost you before in the lies. I don't want to lose you now in the truth.'

Jules felt tears come to her eyes as he put a hand on her arm.

'I know you'll have a lot to deal with, and maybe you won't be ready for another relationship for a while,' Frederick continued. 'I don't even know if that's what I'm saying. But Jules, through everything – through all of my guilt, the pain I've felt, and all I have seen and done – I never stopped thinking about you. My feelings for you – my *love* for you – never changed. That's what caused me so much confusion. Trying to reconcile what I did with how I felt.' He paused once more. 'I'm sorry if this is too much. But, well, if I can't tell you this now, then when can I tell you?'

His words curled around her, casting a glow within her. She didn't want to move; didn't want to breathe. She only wanted to stay still and let them continue to light her. It might have been years ago. She might have been young. But she had loved Frederick – so much. It had taken her a while to realise it; to be ready to push Harry away. But she had, and then when Frederick had left, that feeling hadn't died. It had been shoved down deep, buried by the darkness and dullness of the years that followed, but it had remained. It was growing now, and she wasn't going to push it down or bury it any longer. She wanted to be in the light of his love... in the light of their love.

She'd leaned even closer, so close she thought she could hear his heart pounding.

'I love you too,' she'd said at last.

She stretched in bed, smiling as she took in Frederick's sleeping face.

'Good morning.' His eyes opened as if he'd felt her gaze, and he put an arm around her.

She fit her body against his, remembering that morning so long ago when she'd woken up in this villa, expecting to see this same man beside her and hearing he was gone. She winced, remembering the pain and disbelief when Vannie had told her he'd left. She still couldn't believe everything Vannie had done to keep her secrets hidden.

She pushed aside the sadness and anger. Vannie was gone. She'd left with the paramedics yesterday. Jules had watched her go from the upstairs window, her heart twisting. Vannie had been her best friend for over twenty years, but what kind of friend had she really been? True friends didn't lie and deceive you – and they didn't allow you to live a lie either.

Dread flashed through her at the thought of what lay ahead with Harry – the divorce, telling her father, selling the house... Frederick had wanted to call the police and tell them what had happened, but Jules had shaken her head. How would they even begin to prove that Harry was to blame? He hadn't locked them in there. He may have had the key ring, but he hadn't had the key that had set them free. The truth was that although he may have wanted them to drown, he hadn't been the only one to play a role in keeping them trapped.

Her heart squeezed when she thought of the look on the twins' faces when she'd told them that Harry had left. Mia had refused to believe it, and Nat had run to the annex and refused to come out. How would they feel when they found out that Harry wasn't their father, and Ivy wasn't their half-sister? It would take a lot of time and understanding, and it wouldn't be easy. Hell, she knew herself how hard it was to accept the truth. Part of her had known for years that Harry hadn't loved her, but it had been easier to brush it aside and carry on living. Well, half-living, anyway, because you couldn't call those years actually living.

But that was over. She was going to find a new life, and she couldn't wait. She smiled at Frederick, loving how those piercing blue eyes seemed to *see* her in a way no one else did. It was funny how her fresh start was happening in the same place where she'd thought their chapter had ended. Never in a million years could she have predicted that. No matter how her life had fallen apart – and it had, in a spectacular way – she was going to hang on to what was important to her now: love, happiness and a life that was real.

There was a knock at the door, and Jules sat up in bed. 'One second!' she called out, glancing at Frederick. She didn't want the twins to catch her in bed with someone else so soon after Harry had left, even if nothing had happened. They had enough to contend with. She pulled on a T-shirt and jeans while Frederick went into the en-suite, then opened the door.

It was Ivy, her face pale. Those piercing blue eyes she'd inherited from Frederick seemed bluer than ever.

'Everything OK?' Jules asked, worried. Despite trying to talk to them, the twins had refused to say a word to her last night. Hopefully, neither of them had done anything silly.

'Grandpa's on the phone.' Ivy held out the mobile towards her. 'He said he's been trying to ring you all morning.'

'Oh.' Jules bit her lip and reached out for the phone. What could it be now?

'Hi, Dad,' she said. 'Sorry I didn't answer. It's been quite a time here.'

'I'm afraid I've got some bad news to share, darling.' Her father's voice was heavy. 'Harry was arrested this morning.'

'What? Arrested? For what?' Had someone else here told the police what had happened?

'I didn't want to have to tell you this,' her dad said. 'But Harry has been taking money from the company. For investments, he said. I don't know much, but I think it was some kind of property project overseas. It sounds like he got in with the wrong people, and he'd promised them a lot.'

Wow. Jules breathed out slowly. That was why he'd been so desperate.

'Anyway, I gave him a chance to try to sort it out. I even went against the board and said if he could return the money –

or at least part of it, with a plan to continue payments – by the end of the week, then we wouldn't press charges. It was a huge sum of money, but I wanted to give him a shot... for you, really, and for Ivy. He wouldn't have his job, but at least he wouldn't have a criminal record. Well, not here, anyway.' He sighed. 'But the board hadn't heard anything from him, and their patience ran out. They contacted the police, and the police picked him up at your home this morning.' He paused again. 'It looked like he was packing for a rather long trip. I wanted you to be the first to know. I'm sorry.'

'It's not your fault,' Jules said. The words hung in the air around her. Because while this wasn't his doing, her father had also played a part in this whole tragedy. If he hadn't cheated on her mother, her family would still be intact. The idyllic life would have remained.

But had it been idyllic? It couldn't have been, if her father had cheated – with Vannie, of all people, a young woman who'd seen him as a father figure. Nausea rose at the thought that he could do that. Maybe, like her own marriage, she'd only seen what she'd wanted until the brutal truth was hammered home.

'I'll see you when I'm home, Dad. Talk soon.' Jules hung up. No matter how upset she was, he was still her father. And she'd seen how he'd suffered after her mother's death. She understood even more now why, given the guilt he must have been feeling.

Frederick came to stand beside her. 'What's happened?'

'Harry's been arrested.' She blinked, trying to picture Harry in prison. While it may not be for what he'd done to her, it felt right that he had some consequences for his actions.

Frederick put an arm around her, then a hand on Ivy's arm. They stood there for a minute, just the three of them, as the sun streamed through the window and onto them, banishing the darkness of yesterday's storm... banishing the darkness of past events. It felt like the villa itself was embracing them, bathing them in a circle of light.

'Taxis are coming in half an hour!' Ellie's voice floated up from downstairs.

Jules smiled. It was time to go. To leave this place which had ripped them apart and brought them together once more. Time to go home – to make a new home – and to live the life she should have had, if only things had been different. If only *she* had been different.

'We'll be ready!' she shouted back, then turned to get started.

'Three, two, one, go!' Ellie blew the air horn, shielding her eyes from the summer sunshine as she watched the runners start the 10-kilometre fun run she'd organised to raise money for Jules's new refugee family-tracing service. She couldn't help grinning as Nat and Mia lurched by with perfectly matching scowls. They'd been less than enthusiastic, but Ivy had encouraged them to come. The past couple of months hadn't been easy for them after finding out Harry wasn't their father, but Ivy had kept in contact. They might not have the same dad, she'd said, but she still counted them as family.

Family. Warmth surged through Ellie as she thought of hers. Ivy was right: it was more than biological bonds. Ahmed was her son, biological or not. He'd been so brave to tell her how he'd taken the key and, at first, she hadn't been able to believe it. But when he explained why, she'd understood. She'd been worried too – even after years together, she'd been anxious about the strength of her family's bond. It made sense that Ahmed would be fearful, but she was so proud that in the end, he was secure enough to tell the truth... like Victoria had been, and like she had been in her relationship.

Instead of falling apart as she'd feared, every day their family was growing stronger. Victoria and Ahmed had started doing things on their own together – Victoria had even taken Ahmed out on training runs with her to prepare for this event. Ellie grinned, thinking that sometimes it was more of an excuse to sneak off to McDonald's instead of running around the park, but as long as they were having fun, she didn't mind.

She waved as Safet flashed by, feeling the surge of attraction as she took in his fit physique and chiselled features. He'd been reserved when they'd returned from the villa, but this time she knew to let him be... to let him come to her when he was ready. It hadn't been long until he'd taken her in his arms one night, and things between them were better than ever. Now that she trusted him and his love – now that he knew what she'd kept from him – their relationship felt solid and secure. They'd even been to Bosnia to meet Safet's cousin and his family, and they were getting things ready for them to come and stay.

'It's a great turnout. Thank you so much.' Jules put a hand on her arm, then shielded her eyes to look out at the crowd. 'I can't even see Frederick with all of those runners. Hope he's OK.'

'He's probably at the front of the pack,' Ellie said. 'I'm so pleased he could be here for this.'

Jules smiled. 'Me too. He had a lot of business to tie up in Vietnam, but he's going to be here now for the next few months. I'm really looking forward to spending time with him, and getting the chance to see where this can go.'

'I'm happy for you both.' Ellie stared out at the runners again, her mind spinning. She was happy, but she wished those years Jules and Frederick had to endure without each other hadn't happened... that the horrific events at the villa hadn't happened, both past and present. But maybe all of that had brought them to a place where they could be stronger than ever, like it had with her and Safet.

The reunion *had* brought them together, although it hadn't quite been in the way she'd expected.

'Have you heard from Vannie at all?' She almost didn't want to ask, but she was curious. Jules had told her that Harry was out on bail awaiting trial, but she hadn't said a word about Vannie.

'No. I'm not ready yet. I'm not sure I'll ever be, to be honest.' Sadness slid over Jules's face. 'Ivy has been in touch with her, though.' She sighed. 'I wish Harry had never found out about the affair. He never could have used it as power over Vannie, and everything could have been so different. For both me and her.' Jules looked out at the runners. 'But in the end, I am on the path to have the life I wanted. I hope that someday she can be too. I hope at least she can have some peace.'

Ellie nodded, gazing again at the runners. That was exactly what she felt: that she was at peace with herself; that she had a future she was excited to grasp – to shape with her family. She watched the runners surge forward, disappearing around a curve in the road. You never could be sure what lay ahead. But whatever came, she was strong enough to face it.

After the villa, she believed that more than ever.

A LETTER FROM LEAH MERCER

Dear reader,

I want to say a huge thank you for choosing to read *The Summer Reunion*. If you enjoyed it, and you want to keep up to date with all my latest releases, just sign up at the following link. Your email address will never be shared and you can unsubscribe at any time.

www.bookouture.com/leah-mercer

I hope you loved *The Summer Reunion*. If you did, I would be very grateful if you could write a review. I'd love to hear what you think. It makes such a difference helping new readers to discover one of my books for the first time.

I really enjoy hearing from my readers – you can get in touch through social media or my website.

Thanks,

Leah

www.leahmercer.com

facebook.com/AuthorLeahMercer

x.com/leahmercerbooks

ACKNOWLEDGEMENTS

Thank you to Hannah Todd for her continuing guidance and professionalism. Thanks, also, to Billi-Dee Jones and the amazing Bookouture team for their enthusiasm and hard work to get my books into readers' hands. And, of course, a huge thanks to my readers, reviewers and everyone who has supported me in my writing career.

PUBLISHING TEAM

Turning a manuscript into a book requires the efforts of many people. The publishing team at Bookouture would like to acknowledge everyone who contributed to this publication.

Audio
Alba Proko
Sinead O'Connor
Melissa Tran

Commercial
Lauren Morrissette
Hannah Richmond
Imogen Allport

Contracts
Peta Nightingale

Cover design
Jo Thomson

Data and analysis
Mark Alder
Mohamed Bussuri

Printed in the USA
CPSIA information can be obtained
at www.ICGtesting.com
LVHW042030270924
792325LV00037B/606